STREET ROYALTY 937

STREET ROYALTY 937

I'm So Sincere

Adonte P.M. Cherry

AuthorHouse™
1663 Liberty Drive
Bloomington, IN 47403
www.authorhouse.com
Phone: 1-800-839-8640

© 2012 by Adonte P.M. Cherry. All rights reserved.

No part of this book may be reproduced, stored in a retrieval system, or transmitted by any means without the written permission of the author.

Published by AuthorHouse 04/11/2012

ISBN: 978-1-4685-8368-7 (sc)
ISBN: 978-1-4685-8367-0 (e)

Any people depicted in stock imagery provided by Thinkstock are models, and such images are being used for illustrative purposes only.
Certain stock imagery © Thinkstock.

This book is printed on acid-free paper.

Because of the dynamic nature of the Internet, any web addresses or links contained in this book may have changed since publication and may no longer be valid. The views expressed in this work are solely those of the author and do not necessarily reflect the views of the publisher, and the publisher hereby disclaims any responsibility for them.

Dedications

This book is for all the "Educated Thugs" who did a bid and came out a better man. Also to Jason Henderson, Rob Moore, and Roosevelt Brown (better known as Henny-Pimpin-and-Dust Dawg) respectfully. They were Street Royalty as well. Rest in Peace. To my Old Earth Michelle, who made me the man I am today. To my children who are the inspiration behind my existence. To my daughters mothers who never allowed my time behind the G-Wall to destroy my bond with my princess. Especially Fran who made me want to be a better man. To my sons mothers Erika who brought into existence one greater than I. Thank You! To my block 5542 better known as "The JL" stand up and let's get it how we live. Shout out to anybody that was in contact with me during the 78 months I was gone. We made each other better people and helped each other grow and that will never change . . . . PEACE

This book is a result of a vivid
imagination and should be viewed
as such. All characters are fictional
any similarities in names, situations,
cities, states, etc . . . . are all coincidences.

Foreword

This book in no way, shape, form or fashion was written to glorify a savage lifestyle. Nor to disrespect the teachings of the 5% Nation of God's and Earth. This story is fictional and shows and proves that a person can have knowledge (know) of the lessons and be able to speak wisdom and the lessons, yet still have no understanding (true image) of the lessons. Therefore they cannot deal in equality because they are still savage in their pursuit of happiness. The 5% are righteous people who aren't Pro Black nor Anti White, we are about teaching the babies. Many of us come from the street life and even after receiving the knowledge of Self still dwell in the street life out of a sense of loyalty to which we came from. If this book does anything I hope it's to motivate all the true "G" stuck on these modern day plantations known as prisons to get knowledge of self so you can teach your seeds a much better way out. That's the only way to slow down the prison population that's become the new Black community.

Much love and respect to those who did time and became better men. Malcolm X 7 years, Father Allah 22 months, Abu Shahid 7 plus years, Marcus Garvey 5 years, George Jackson life and even hustlers like Don King! You all changed lives and altered history in a positive way after becoming prisoners. P.E.A.C.E

Chapter 1

2004

"A Flick, where you at bra?" Monster said ridin down Salem Avenue in his black Tahoe on 26 inch rims.

"I'm in the hood", Flick started but Monster cut him off.

"I just came from downtown at the Justice Center ni$$a" Monster stated emphatically.

"Ni$$a just chill, we'll talk when you get to the hood. I'm over Talacie's house, so come through". Flick told Monster just as Monster said "It's on" and hung up.

Speeding up a little over the speed limit Monster lit up a blunt of silver haze hoping to calm his nerves. He couldn't think straight for shit, everything was a distraction so he turned his music off to see if that'd help any. Detective Hicks had boxed him and Flick in on a body they had nothing to do with. They had a good idea who had though and he knew it too. Detective Hicks was a dirty ass detective who had been born and raised in the Dayton and Springfield area, so he knew almost everyone and everything. He was one of the most feared detectives around, he extorted majority of the hustlers and robbed the rest. He was a cold hearted muthafucka and now he was at Flick and Monster.

Now as Monster rode in his truck trying to comprehend what he'd just agreed to and what Flick had already agreed to, he knew shit was about to get real crazy . . .

Talacie stood in her doorway as Monster got out of his truck. "What's good ni$$a . . . You aight"., she asked looking him up and down.

"Yeah what up", Monster responded brushing past Talacie's chocolate ass.

Talacie was a cute little hood hoe who was fucking anybody who's paper was right. Her house was a true trap spot where you could stash guns; cook and sale work, or fuck other hood hoe's. As soon as Monster entered the kitchen his mood was detected by his partner.

"Don't let that shit stress you ni$$a", Flick said sitting at the table rolling a blunt as Monster sat across from him.

"What the fuck you mean . . . ni$$a we gotta testify if he go to trial". Monster said.

"Just think about it like this . . . You know them JL ni$$a is laying down every ni$$a eating and extorting muthafuckas too. Why you think that ni$$a been coming to the city bra?" Flick asked, then nodded "Plus Hicks got it out for us about that one shit . . . It's either us or him ni$$a and I ain't going down."

"You right my ni$$a but damn Sin."

"Fuck Sin . . . Fuck that hoe ass ni$$a and the rest of them JL ni$$a's . . . Somebody should've been got at them ni$$a's." Flick yelled as he got up and paced back and forth past the kitchen sink.

"Ni$$a we going to court if we have to and that's that." Flick told Monster as he calmed down enough to light his blunt . . .

"Stop boy . . . Nah I ain't fucking with young ass." Talacie said from the next room. Flick and Monster glanced at each before Monster spoke out.

"Who's is that?" He asked

"It's me ni$$a," Elan said as he entered the kitchen. Elan was just another young ni$$a off the block who couldn't get over the hump, keeping the same ole grams. Just enough to cop his shoes, gear, and a smoke sack of dro and then re-up again.

"What up?" Flick said as he moved towards the cabinet where he kept his ounces at.

"I got $600 bra . . . Can I get one for that?" Elan asked

"$650 an ounce young'n you know what it is . . ." Flick told Elan as he grabbed a ounce of crack and a digital scale from the cabinet.

"Let me own you $50 on my next trip . . . I'm fucked up right now bra." Elan told Flick but looked at Monster knowing he was the better one to deal with when you needed a deal. Flick just gave Elan a blank stare as if to say "don't fuck wit my money," before he handed over the work that he'd just weighted in at 29.2 grams with the bag. Hitting the blunt then passing it to Monster he sat back down to count the $600 as Elan left Talacie's house . . .

Chapter 2

"Okay then nephew . . . How long you been out?" Stevie Day asked Sin as he opened his door like a neighborhood valet parker.

"Almost 6 months unc . . . What's good wit chu?" Sin asked as he looked left to right to survey the hood he'd left over 2 years ago.

"Ain't nothin nephew . . . Glad to see you home." Stevie Day said as he threw his hands to Sin and called out a cadence of punches.

"Now that's what I'm talkin about nephew . . . I see you still sharp with that 4 piece off the jab."

"You know I stay on point unc I was putting them lames down in there."

"Yeah nephew I know how you roll so put me down . . . I wanna be with the man who got the crown." Stevie said as he danced around like him and Sin were in a ring.

I'm rotating elsewhere unc . . . But you know what it is when I get back to it . . . I'ma find you." Sin said as he reached for his phone to see who was calling him. Sin noticed Cat's number so he leaned back against his Infinity G35 Coup which he kept plain Jane to avoid the attention.

"Peace. What's jumping little mama?"

"I ain't heard shit but I got one of them ni$$as numbers." Cat told Sin.

"Ok ma . . . Which one?" Sin asked

"The Kev ni$$a who be with T.J, he drive a white LHS." Cat said

"Yeah, yeah what's the number?"

"520-0012"

"Good lookin ma, I'm back at you in a minute." Sin told Cat then hung up. After 15 minutes Sin told unc to hold it down as he jumped in his Coup and pulled off with money on his mind.

Sin had just got out of prison and nothing looked pretty, his hood and his homie's were all looking bad. Reality was beginning to show its ugly face. Unlike his first month or so out, truth was beginning to shine like the light its symbolic too. The truth about his closes JL partners, the truth about his baby mother's and the rest of his family. He'd known most of the people in his hood since free lunch and everything looked good from a distance but the closer he got to the truth, the brighter the light shined. Sin knew he had to face reality that nobody had grew in his absence and it was on him to bring it back home to the hood he loved . . . Taking heed to the obstacles ahead of himself Sin rode around Springfield focusing on his plans. Sin knew plenty of ways to get money, he kept ten different hustle's but whenever in these streets all he knew was to go hard. Sin had always been a "Go-Getta" and had a magnetic like attraction to making profit so although he had plans on lay'n low, spending time with his seeds and starting a record label to put out his and his little homie's music, he had to get his money right first. Sin dreaded it but he knew he'd have to snatch up some of that fast money via extortion, home invasion or flipping bricks. He had a nice flow on the mic, his charisma always shined and his delivery was unique as fuck. The entire time he was on lock he went hard on the writing aspect to perfect his craft. He had 1000's of sixteens he could convert to song form and he wanted to put his shit out. Every weekend on the yard Sin would battle ni$$as from other cities, he never lost, he'd even recorded a few song's on the cheap ass penitentiary equipment. Ni$$as was always running around reciting Sin's verses on the way to chow, rec, shit even visits. He knew he was nice but all that was on hold for now.

Between living the street life and traveling back and forth to Charlotte, NC to spend time with his youngest daughter Asia and her mother Naomi, Sin had ran through over $100,000 cash. Add that to the fact that his lawyer was lay'n back suckin up his funds and Sin's back was against the wall when he came home . . . Standing 5'7 and only weighing 155lbs, Sin was small in size but his name always hit like a heavy weight. His older brother was gone on the 1 year bid to Madison Correctional but it had been close to 4 years since they'd seen each other. No matter how long the time it always seemed to start when one was getting out causing them to miss each other. Azon was 3 years older than Sin and a total opposite. Sometimes Sin wondered how two people born of the same womb and raised by the same mother could have different outlooks on life. Azon had started getting locked up as a teenager. He gang banged, sold crack and even had a few assaults before they finally laid his young ass down in Tico Juvenile Facility in Columbus Ohio. While doing 18 months in Tico, Azon had made the mistake of telling Sin where he hid his gun. Sin was only 13 years old but as soon as he laid his hands on the 2 shot Dillinger, that fit in the palm of his little hand, he was fiening to feel it fire off a round. Ever since that first surge of power rushed threw Sin at 13 he loved busting guns.

Being a middle child, Sin understood that his younger brother Donta looked up to him, similar to how he did Azon. This kept Sin from wilding out unnecessarily, although they were a year apart Donta and Sin were alike, but oh so different. While they aged into young men, Sin attempted to master both worlds, that of the educated and that of the thugs. Donta stayed away from the streets. Other than stopping through the hood to shoot dice, talk shit or slap box, Donta stayed busy with school or working some job. He'd already received a Bachelor's Degree in Criminal Justice, which enabled him to work as a juvenile probation officer but he decided to go back for his Masters Degree. Sin was proud of his little brother and was always there to put up all the money whenever Donta put on his youth clinics for under privileged kids. Sin knew how important it was for the kids in his hood and all around the city to have summer camps like Donta's to keep them off the streets. At 25 years old Sin had committed every crime short of rape or murder gaining him much deserved fear and respect throughout Ohio as well as general status in his hood, but he still had the morals his mother instilled into him and his brothers. With Sin being the middle of the three boys he received less attention than Donta, but more than Azon. Gifted in sports and skilled at macking hoes Sin had great promise to live up too. But with a heart as big as Texas and pride to match Sin stayed in some shit that him bustin his four-five.

Chapter 3

On the regular Sin wasn't no robbery boy, but it was clear that ni$$as in the hood ain't have shit going on and he'd lost his Arizona connect while he was locked up. Sin was hungry so he had it set in his mind to go get it. Life was like chess and he was a true king. He knew how to utilize all his pieces from a pawn to a queen. They all had to protect the king. He'd been laying on a few ni$$as that was eatin. Doing his homework on who fucked with who, who was whose connect and who's main bitch played in these streets. Sin had a down ass bitch name Cat from the west side of Dayton. She was a fly caramel complexioned shorty that was thick all the way down to her ankles. For Sin, she was down for anything, so he knew she'd help get that paper outta ni$$as. She'd already been fucking anybody who was getting paper throughout Springfield and Dayton. Getting her bills paid by performing her deep throat oral skills. She had a stint as a stripper at a club name * Fields Finest* that was owned by Sin's man Rob "Pimpin" Moore on the south side of Springfield. Cat was a dime piece in every sense of the word physically, but mentally she had no sense of self worth. After six solid months at *Fields Finest* she'd built up enough clientele to have her regulars just drop cash on hotel suites when they wanted to get sucked and fucked.

Being the man that Sin was tended to be hard at times. He had love for Cat and never understood how a woman so crazy sexy could allow herself to be ran through sexually the way she did. She had the power over weak ni$$as but instead of embracing it she choose to diminish it, after all Sin thought her pussy had to be worn out by now . . . Cat also had a son name Seven who was 11 years old. Sin paid Seven a lot of attention, making sure he was up on the game of life out here in these streets and making sure he was well taken care of. Seven looked up to Sin, so he was all ears whenever Sin spoke to him and all eyes when he seen Sin around. Seven wanted to be just like Sin when he grew up but he could never understand why Sin would always tell him he could tell he'd be better than him when he was older.

Sin had never heard of or seen Seven's father and at times he'd wondered if he was his father. Although Cat had denied it Sin still wondered. Sin met Cat in 1993 when he was 13 years old and soon after was fucking whenever her parents went to work. Sin had been fucking Cat over a year when all of sudden her sent her to live in Dayton. Now here they were 12 years after first meeting and Sin still had her total loyalty. Cat had been in love with Sin since they'd met but also blamed him for her promiscuous ways, claiming she only did extraordinary shit like threesomes when she was with him. Only a fool would believe that and Sin had never been a fool but letting her think he believed her was his way of rocking her to sleep. Besides Cat always came through for Sin and her latest move was right on time . . . .

Cat had been fucking with this lame ni$$a name T.J. for about 4 months now so he'd gotten real comfortable with her and stopped taking her to hotels, hitting his stash house instead. That made this lick as simple as possible and soon as T.J. called

Cat today saying he was coming to get her, she called Sin. When they got to the stash house Cat fucked and sucked T.J. until he fell asleep, then sent Sin a text with the address in it. It only took one shot into the pillow next to this ni$$a's head to get him to come up off of half a brick of cocaine and $24,000 cash . . . .

Two days later Sin was on the JL getting ready to turn the half a brick of coke into a whole brick so he could just dump four nine packs on a few of his lil homies at $6,000 s piece, when he finally heard from Cat.

"Damn ma you had me worried that, that clown done murked you or something" Sin said soon as he heard Cat's voice.

"That pussy ass ni$$a ain't suspect nothing . . . Besides he softer than a baby's ass". Cat said laughing at Sin's worry.

"Ok ma I see you feeling yourself . . . So when you gone come down here and get this money?"

"I'll be by later tonight . . . Give me 2 hours." Cat responded before they hung up.

Getting back to business Sin walked into the kitchen where Nene and Missy were fast at work breaking down the ounces of fishscale cocaine before putting it into the coffee grinder to turn it to a dust form so it could mix with the anisitol powder. Smacking Nene on her nice round ass that was swallowing the thong she stood there in, Sin asked.

"Was there enough acetone for the whole brick?"

"Yeah baby it's all good" . . .

"Nine are in the oven now." Nene said pointing towards the oven where Missy stood butt naked watching the timer carefully. Nene turned on the grinder and Sin stepped back to enjoy the back side view of his two hood hoes, one naked and one only in a thong as they whipped up his work. Sin had to laugh inside; he had been fucking both of these hoes since he came home. They hated each other at one point in time but after soaking up Sin's smooth game, they agreed to share when it came to Sin. Now here they were working together and it was a beautiful site to see . . . After all the ounces were bagged up and stashed away Sin told Nene and Missy he couldn't fuck with them tonight cause he had to move this work. Knowing Cat was coming through tonight he wasn't pressed to fuck either of his hood hoes. They both had some good pussy but their head game was no match for Cat's . . . After Sin's hood hoes had left, Sin sat back to watch an episode of the "Wire" on his projector that fed to a 91 inch screen along the wall. Just as he got settled, Cat hit his chirp saying she was enroute and to give her ½ an hour. It took about 45 minutes to get from her house in the Upper View section of Dayton to the JL in Springfield, so Sin knew she had to already be beyond half way here to say half an hour. Cat always knew coming to the JL to take precautionary measures like unnecessary stops, circling the block and even pulling into a fake driveway or two. Sin trained all his hoes, baby momma's and wifey to be careful but Cat excelled cause she was a set up bitch to begin with. When Cat finally chirped for Sin to open the door, he grabbed his chopper and went to the dark hallway adjacent the houses entrance after he'd unlocked it from the dark hallway he couldn't be seen but had a perfect view of the entrance. This was a precaution Sin always took just in case someone was outside waiting and had snatched Cat up to come in with her. Sin had long ago mastered The 33 Strategies Of War and knew the king had to protect his castle at all cost. Cat knew to knock 7 times, then enter if she wasn't in danger, so after counting 7 knocks then seeing the door open barely enough to allow Cat's sexy frame to squeeze in he knew shit was all good. Cat locked the door behind her, then went into the living room and sat down. Knowing Sin wasn't coming out for a few more minutes she started to count the money sitting on the table.

"What the fuck you doing counting my money ma?" Sin barked at Cat as he entered the room. Cat was shocked so she looked up quickly and nervously only to breathe easy when she seen the grin on Sin's face. "Damn ma you scared to death."

"Ain't nobody scared of you Sincere." Cat said as she sat the money back on the table.

"Then why you put the money back down then?" Sin asked as he stepped in front of Cat within arms reach. Cat was a little confused so she shook her head no and told Sin that was way more than she was to get."

"That's all you ma, nine stacks . . . I'm upping your cut so you can fall back a minute . . . I'm home now so you don't have to take unnecessary risk or fuck with miscellaneous muthafucka's out here. As long as you stay down for me, I'm make sure you and Seven live nice." Sin told Cat.

Times like this reminded Cat of why she'd loved Sin so long. Reaching out she grabbed Sin by the belt and pulled him even closer while staying seated. Sin knew what was about to go down so felt his dick start to rock up. By the time Cat had his pants and boxers down his dick sprung out like a jack in the box. Cat smiled up at Sin as she massaged his shaft till it stretched all the way out, then she stuck out her tongue and gave a few good lollipop style licks to his head . . .

"Oh shit . . . Damn ma you missed this dick huh?" Sin asked not looking for a reply. Cat was getting into what she's excellent at so a "Um hmm" was all the response she could give anyways. Licking down Sin's dick and softly sucking on his balls before returning back to his dick, she took pride in making Sin feel good but tonight she really wanted to show her appreciation with her felicitous head game.

"Damn ma . . . Oh yeah . . . Right there." Sin whispered as he ran his hand across Cat's short hair. Sucking on Sin's head and jacking the base of his dick while looking up, Cat was on her job and they both loved it. The sensations felt so good Sin began to fuck Cat's face faster encouraging her to deep throat all 9 plus inches. Cat knew Sin would blow his load soon so she sped up and let his dick touch the back of her throat each time before pulling back. Sin was there and Cat knew it so she pulled his dick out long enough to look up at Sin with her sexy ass brown eyes.

"Let me swallow all your cum." She begged. Holding her gaze she slid her lips back down his dick, working her tongue all around his head. That was it took, feeling his load travel up his rod Sin grabbed the back of Cat's head and shot his nut in the back of her throat. Being the pro she is Cat kept sucking and swallowing at the same time till Sin's knee's buckled and he pulled back in surrender.

"I see you still can't handle my head?" Cat asked giggling then licking her lips and saying "Oh you taste so good." After pulling up his pants and flopping down on the couch, Sin just sat there and smiled at Cat's silly ass thinking "this my rider till the wheels fall off" . . .

Chapter 4

When Sin awoke in the morning he grabbed his phone to check the time and see if he'd missed any calls. It was close to 11:00am so Sin hopped up and called Sunday to tell her he was on his way out there. Sin was alone cause Cat had left around 4:00am she never stayed all night and Sin had no problem with that. Sin rushed his shower so he could gather up tha brick of coke Nene and Missy had manufactured last night. Sin never kept work on the JL for more than 24 hours, it was too hot in his hood. The police were always liable to come banging on the door looking for anyone of Sin's family members. Sunday stayed in a nice little one bedroom apartment Sin had put her up in, she was 2 months pregnant. Sin had never met Sunday's family but they'd heard so much crazy shit about him that they tried to keep Sunday away by sending her to a suburban village to live with her uncle. Sunday had been Sin's pinch hitter for 5 years prior to her getting pregnant so their connection was much stronger than her mother had known. After only a month she'd reached out to Sin to bring her back . . . Nobody knew where Sunday lived nor that the baby she was carrying was Sin's other than family. Sin always took careful and extended routes to her apartment in case someone tried to follow him. As he parked he called and told Sunday to unlock the door, cocking his baby glock .40 and placing it in his jacket pocket Sin hopped out his G35 coupe. Sin stayed on point for any robbery attempt. With the bag in his left hand and his right hand holding his glock inside his pocket. Sin trotted in the building. Sunday stayed on the bottom floor so Sin took a quick left soon as he entered the complex. Walking through the door Sin greeted Sunday with "Peace Isis. What's up?"

"Nothing just waiting on you." Sin replied as she grabbed Sin's hand pulling him to the bedroom. "Woo woo. Hold up ma . . . Let me put this work up." Sin told Sunday as he turned to dead bolt the door.

"Well you better hurry up before I start without you." Sunday said pulling off the Educated Thug Wear tee shirt she had on to reveal that was naked underneath. Sunday sexily walked towards the bedroom while Sin rushed to toss the work in the closet and follow her swaying hips. Sunday was America's Next Top Model material from head to toe and even after giving birth Sin was gonna encourage her to pursue a modeling career. But as he looked at her sitting in the edge of her bed he was actually glad he was the only one with the privilege of seeing this beautiful site . . . Sin started to question Sunday but she cut him off saying

"Daddy be quiet and let me take care of you."

Sin allowed Sunday to undress him quickly and lay him down on the bed, sitting next to him Sunday started to rub, lick and kiss all over Sin's body. Making her way to his lips she sucked on them hungrily as they kissed. After a minute or so she turned around so her ass could face Sin while she sucked his dick. Taking Sin's dick in her mouth Sunday started to suck all the way down then back up. Just as it got good Sin reached up and started to rub Sunday's pussy from the back, her pussy was soaking wet and Sin rubbed all in between her lips causing her to speed up on his dick making loud slurping sounds. Sin was damn there ready to bust so he told Sunday "slow down ma or I'm bout to cum." Not wanting Sin to cum Sunday stopped sucking and climbed on top of Sin backwards. Sin's dick slid right in Sunday's super wet pussy and she slid down his length real slow while rubbing her own clit. After her ass cheeks were square on Sin's lower stomach and all his dick inside her Sin grabbed her hips and lifted her up and down on his dick with force. Sunday was unable to speak so she moaned in ecstasy as she started cumming hard. Sunday's pussy started throbbing around Sin's dick but he didn't wanna cum yet so he flipped her over and put her right leg up by her head. Sticking his dick back in only half way Sin grabbed her hair with his free hand so she couldn't move.

"You ready ma?" Sin asked as he held his dick still in her pussy that felt like warm water."

"Yes . . . Give it to me now." Sunday responded as she tried to move her hip's toward Sin. Sin knew how she wanted it so he started pounding her pussy fast and hard with long strokes. Still unable to move Sunday took all Sin delivered and screamed "Harder . . . Harder. Fuck me hard."

After a good 5 minutes Sunday was out of breath and cumming again before Sin finally pulled out and bust his nut on top of her pussy so she can rub it all over her clit just how she liked it. An hour later Sin sat in the front room watching Sports Center while Sunday slept sedated from the long dick'n she'd received earlier. Getting into deep thought Sin pondered about the acts that had changed his life 2 and a half years ago . . . .

Chapter 5

2 years prior . . .

Dressed in all black State Property attire, black Newman football gloves and a black Cincinnati fitted hat Sin gripped his Beretta 9mm and inserted its extended 30 round clip. Placing the gun on his lap Sin pulled into the lot of Qualities Corner store that was ran by Sam and his Arabian family. Sin had knew Sam since he was 10 years old so whenever he put in work at Qualities he knew he'd be good and protected from the police. Sam always either erased the tapes or conveniently lost them whenever something went down. Sin was cool, calm, comfortable and ready to get that paper when he pulled up next to a light gray F150 pick up truck. The owner, Kent was a old head who'd been flipping bricks and pounds of weed for over 10 years now. He'd did a little Fed time on a tax evasion case but he'd only met new better connects while down. Kent was definitely still spending money from 1996, he was probably the last ni$$a with small face hundred dollar bills in Springfield. Kent had known Sin's mother, aunts and uncle since they'd moved here from Philly before Sin was even born. As Sin stepped out his cherry red drop top 68 Impala on 24 inch rims, Kent said,

"What up young playa."

"A new era . . . That's what's up." Sin said raising his Beretta towards Kent's face.

"Time to pay taxes old man."

"Come on lil Sin you can't be serious . . . You gone do me like this. You really bout what you try'n to do?" Kent asked Sin in an attempt to either reason with him or scare him outta what he was doing.

"Where you stashin it at bitch?" Sin asked still holding a steady aim at Kent's face, continuing to try and plead Kent said,

"You serious little ni$$a you . . . But Sin cut his talk short by busting two rounds into Kent's rear truck window.

"What you need youngsta? We can make this right." Kent pleaded with fear beginning to creep into his eyes. Sin was focused and already had his plans in order so he told Kent to move over in the truck so they could take a ride. As they pulled out the lot Sin called Sam and told him to watch his car for about an hour till he got back. Sin had Kent turn on MLK Blvd and head north before making a call to his partner Born Cipher who was at Kent's wife house in the Mallory Court's section of Dayton.

"Peace to the God." Born Cipher said into the phone knowing it was Sin calling.

"Peace God . . . how shit going your way?" Sin asked as he put Born Cipher on speaker phone so Kent could hear every word.

"I got this hoe naked and tied to the bedpost . . . . This bitch got a nice frame . . . I know that old ni$$a ain't fucking this bitch right." Born Cipher said then asked

"So what you want done to the bitch?"

"That depends on old Kent here . . . I just wanted to make sure you had the hoe." Sin said then hung up. Turning to Kent Sin seem reality starting to kick in.

"You know what it is. Take me to that work or your wife's a dead woman." Sin said sticking his gun in Kent's ribcage.

"Ok. Ok . . . I'll do it." Kent yelled in defeat.

Twenty minutes later they were on the outskirts of Springfield off of route 4 that lead to Dayton in front of a big farm style house. Sin had Kent call one of his workers to bring out 5 bricks of raw cocaine and Kent also told him there was $100,000 cash at his wife's house, he claimed he'd just re-up'd and had already set most of it out on consignment. Sin wasn't trippin on the amount he was getting, he was more focused on his plan running smoothly. Sin knew there were camera's all around that house so getting outta the truck was outta the question. He couldn't let Kent live after this cause it'd mean constant war. The worker was this older ni$$a name Flick that Sin knew from around the way. Sin made sure Flick didn't see his face when he brought out the 5 bricks. Sin had Kent drive out to this wooded fishing area where Born Cipher had already dug a shallow grave at the day before. Kent was nervous pulling up to such a secluded area but once he seen another car in the area he relaxed as much as he could, not realizing that the other car had brought his worst nightmare there. After taking Kent's keys out the ignition, Sin hopped out the truck, bag in hand, ran to the other car, got in the driver's seat and drove away. Kent finally felt like he could breathe again, like he'd made it out of this ordeal but before he could gather his thoughts, Born Cipher stepped outta the darkness and blew Kent's head all over his front seats with a .44 magnum.

Chapter 6

It had been 2 months since Cat had set up T.J ni$$a so Sin wasn't surprised when she called talking about this super easy lick she had for him. Sin told her to set it up for 2 days later cause he was in Charlotte with his daughter but he'd be back the next day. Sin wanted this to be his last lick so he hoped this ni$$a had a nice stash or some heavy work. Sin's goal was to hit for a quarter million, then retire from the stick up game altogether, besides he had goons on the way home from the joint who he could leave the game to. He had a long way to go though he thought as he recounted the $39,000 he'd profited off the last lick Cat had set up. Sin put that money back in his safe and returned to the front room where his daughter Asia and her mother Naomi were watching television. Stopping in the doorway Sin admired what he had in front of him and smiled. Sin had met Naomi in 1993 and shot his game at her every chance he got until 1996 when she finally went for it. They had been together ever since, although now it was like they weren't apart but weren't together either. Asia was 6 years old and looked liked her mother but acted like her father. She loved spending time with her daddy and everybody knew it. Naomi and Asia had moved to Charlotte when Asia was 2 years old to be by Naomi's family and Sin had no problem following suit a year later. They got a nice 3 bedroom house on the outskirts of the city and did the family thing till Sin got restless for that street life. Naomi still stuck by Sin cause she knew he was a good man and great father. That's why Sin needed to get this quarter million so they could live happily ever after.

"Why are you looking at us like that silly." Asia said running up and jumping into Sin's arm's.

"Cause I love you and I can look at you how I want to silly willy." Sin said tickling Asia in her sides as he hung on to her.

"Mom help me, momma." Asia cried out in between giggles but her mother wasn't no help and all she could do was take it till her daddy decided to stop. Diving onto the couch with his daughter still in his arms Sin asked her.

"Who loves you?"

"You daddy." was Asia's reply as she kissed her daddy on the cheek. Later that night Sin told Naomi he had to go back to Ohio the next day to handle some business but he'd be back in two weeks tops. He also told her how much money he'd put up and if she needed any to go ahead and get it. Naomi knew what Sin was going home to do, she'd even seen him in action one time back in 1998, she didn't like it but she knew he had goals beyond the streets and the streets were just his medium for now. With understanding in her eyes Naomi kissed Sin softly and told him knowledge every situation and be careful. Sin and Naomi made love for what seemed like hours that night and when Sin awoke in the next morning she was gone to work and his daughter to school . . .

Two days later Sin sat on the JL cleaning his snub nose 38 special which would be his weapon of choice for this lick he was waiting on Cat to call him about. The set up was on point, Cat was over this little ni$$a name Clarky house just like she was every

Thursday night and he was getting ready to move his work from there to another spot like he did every Thursday. After receiving Cat's call Sin hopped in his 87 two door box Chevy and sped off to the east side of Dayton. Fatigued up . . . full of blood. Sin dragged Clarky and the bag of work he was attempting to move back to the house. He knew Clarky had told Cat to never open the door unless he called first. Sin told Clarky to call his ni$$a who was in the house not wanting to let Clarky know he knew it was a bitch in there instead. Clarky tried to play dumb like he ain't have nobody in the house so Sin put his snub nose in Clarky's mouth.

"Bitch if you don't make that call, I'ma blow your fuckin head off."

Sin said as he cocked back the hammer to let Clarky know he was dead serious. Clarky fumbled with his phone then made another attempt to tell Sin this bag was all he had. That was the wrong move, Sin twisted his gun to the side and squeezed the trigger blowing a hold in Clarky's left cheek. Sin grabbed Clarky before he could run away and told him, "make that call or the next shot gonna be straight down your throat." Clarky made the call and although his words were barely audible it was all Cat needed to be cleared of suspicion. Once inside Sin tied Clarky up, made Cat strip and fake tortured her to make Clarky open his safe. Sticking his gun in and out of Cat's pussy and her fake cries was all it took to get this sucka for love to open his safe. Not even bothering to count the money Sin bagged it up and walked out the house like nothing had ever happened. Still amped off the rush of busting his gun Sin noticed he was speeding and had to pull over at the gas station before getting on the highway. Sin snatched off his fatigues and threw on a Educated Thug Wear sweat suit, dumped the fatigues in the trash and proceeded into the gas station to grab a lemonade ice tea and some alcohol pads. Sin flirted with the cashier then hit the highway more relaxed than 5 minutes prior. Forty five minutes later Sin sat on the JL with all the contents from the bag dumped on the floor. He couldn't believe it, this was very possible his last lick. Sin's mind raced as he thought of a plan to assure he could leave the game. Sin counted $60,000 cash and 36 ounces of heroin so he knew he had a chance to retire he just had to master mind it right. Up all night Sin plotted and planned and finally had a blue print laid out. The next day Sin called his man's from New York name Beast cause that heroin game was all Beast fuck with, him and his team from N.Y had been hustling that dog food in Springfield, Dayton and Columbus for years now. Sin told Beast to come through A-Sap so he could run down his plans.

"Peace to the God. What's good whoodi whoo?" Beast said as he walked in the front room on the JL."

"Peace fam. I need your expertise fam." Sin told Beast as he got up to get the bag of work. Sin returned and tossed it to Beast before sitting back down.

"Damn sun, what's this a whole slab?" Beast asked Sin as he pulled out a few ounces.

"Yeah, but I need it to look like 2 whole ones. Can you do that for me?" Sin asked already knowing the answer.

"Most definitely sun we gotta hit the mall so I can cop some shit from GNC but far as the stretching we can do that at my bitch house." Beast told Sin.

Sin could see that Beast was excited but when he left the room and came back tossing Beast five $5000 dollar stacks his excitement escalated.

"That's you fam for handling this for me." Sin told Beast.

"Yo on the really real that's why I fucks with you God, that's real shit. I appreciate the love sun." Beast told Sin as they prepared to leave to go handle business . . .

A few days later Sin finally heard from Cat talking bout how she played her role to a tee and even went to the hospital to be examined. Sin laughed and told her he had $25,000 for her and how he was done and wanted her to be finished too. She was happy about the money but not about him being done, but after 30 minutes of lecturing her on what could happen if she set up the wrong muthafucka Sin finally got Cat to chill till one of his lil homies came to take his place. Sin didn't really have any feelings for Cat but he cared about her well being and even felt responsible for her ways and actions so he didn't want her doing shit without him or one of his comrades. Cat ended up coming by the next day to collect her cash, also to further assure her promise to chill till Sin put her down with someone.

Meanwhile Sin was busy moving the two bricks of heroin he had. It took him a few weeks but when it was all said and done he'd made a cool $200,000 to add with the $10,000 cash and was ready to head down to Charlotte. Sin knew better than to hit the highway with this kind of cash and possibly get pulled over for DWB(Driving While Black) so he called his Spanish Italian mami Nikki. Sin kept a nice stable of women he could count on to handle certain situations and as a driver Nikki always came through cause she could pass for a white girl. Sin set it up to follow her and the money down south the next day. Sin preferred to drive at night so they left at 11:00 pm on Sunday night so they could arrive at 7:00am Monday. No one in Ohio outside of Sin's mother knew where he stayed down south and he kept it that way by having Nikki pull into the Concord Mills parking lot to grab the bag of cash. Concord Mills was a huge mall so there was nothing suspicious about Sin and Nikki pulling in there at 7:00am just like a lot of the managers who were preparing to open their store doors around 8:00am. After parting ways Nikki continued to Miami where she also had a home and Sin headed towards Naomi's in hopes that he'd get there in time to see his daughter before school.

As Sin pulled up Naomi and Asia were coming outta the house so after kissing them both Sin went ahead in the house letting Naomi take their daughter to school. To excited to wait till later, Sin went straight to collect $39,000 from his safe, he then counted and laid out all the money from his bag in stacks of $10,000 a piece until he had 24 stacks laid on the bed and $9,000 in hand. Smiling ear to ear Sin called Naomi to do a little test he knew she'd pass.

"Peace Queen." Sin said in a loving voice when Naomi answered.

"Peace baby, I'm leaving Asia school now, you need me to stop anywhere?" Naomi asked figuring Sin wanted some breakfast or something.

"Yeah baby I need you to let me borrow a thousand dollars, can you stop at the bank and get it?" Sin asked.

"Sin what are you up to now?" Naomi said curiously.

"I just the paid the bills so I only have like $1200 but I'll stop and get you $1000." She continued before he could even answer.

"Ok baby that's Peace. I love you and I'll see you in a little bit." Sin said before they both said "Peace" and hung up. Sin laughed to his self knowing that this $1000 would put him at his $250,000 goal and now he could leave the streets alone . . .

Chapter 7

"It ain't a game,
And if it is I got the cheat codes
Bullets and clips . . .
JL goons keep those,
That's why we infamous,
Robbin, stabbin, shooting muthafuckas,
Come on I ain't gotta get into this
You suckas know what it is,
Specially if you from here,
Bullets hoes and stab wounds,
You can get done here"

Was all you heard as Sin flew up Salem and turned on Grand headed to his oldest daughter's house. Sin had been hitting the studio hard for the past 7 months now and loved to ride around banging his own shit. He felt as good as he did in 2001 when he first started wearing his own clothes. Sin was feeling his self so when he pulled up to a stop sign and seen a dice game jumping off he decided to pull down and stop the bank. Stuntin was always a habit but gambling was his only addiction, ever since Sin had reached his goal he'd been hitting Las Vegas hard to gamble and had even cleaned up some of his dirty money that way. Holding a $5000 cash bankroll out the window Sin pulled up and said "If ya'll playing cee-lo I'm stopping the bank." At first ni$$az looked at his knot with treachery in their eyes, but thought twice when they seen the gun Sin had on his hip.

"Let's get it." One of the ni$$as said halfway bent over with a nice chain hanging off his neck. Sin slid into his Educated Thug Wear hoodie that had a fist gripping money that dripped blood pattern all over it and the words Blood Money embroiled in the chest so he could cover up his gun. He intentionally let his gun be seen at first to make sure any robbery attempt be second guessed. Sin was in his 68 drop Impala on 24's and before he could even find out how much the bank was the ni$$az was asking about his whip. As Sin answered a few quick questions one of the ni$$az kept staring at him.

"Sincere . . . Sincere Wallace." The little ni$$a said curiously. How this muthafuckas know my name Sin thought to his self before asking.

"Yea. How you know my name lil homie?"

"Damn Sin. It is you. What's good bra. I'm Lil Elan." Sin just looked at Elan try'n to recall where he'd knew him from.

"I just know your name from being out here . . . But I also used to be over Kiyla house when you fucked with her . . . I was fucking her lil sister Victoria." Elan rambled on try'n to get Sin to remember him or one of the times he was over Kiyla's. Their conversation had everyone's attention now and even had a few ni$$az remembering stories they'd heard about Sin, their's weren't about no hoes through.

"What up. You still fucking with Kiyla. That bitch bad." Elan said.

"Nah . . . It wasn't like that, I was just fucking here and there, but I ain't seen her in a while." Sin said as he glanced around the crowd of faces to gauge their reactions to his name. Just as they were about to start the game back up a police cruiser hit the corner. The ni$$az who had money on the ground stepped on it while the others including Sin and Elan walked away slowly.

"Damn . . . This bitch clean bra." Elan said looking inside Sin's whip.

"I kinda remember your face . . . You related to Kamadie right?" Sin asked walking to the drivers seat.

"Yea . . . That's my big cousin. Remember I used to be getting my shit braided every time you came through."

"Yea lil homie . . . I know your fam. You was young as fuck when I was slidin that way. How you remember that?" Sin asked lifting up the driver's side door Lamborghini style.

"Cause whenever you came over them hoes would be hype like you was fucking the whole family." Sin laughed at that comment then said

"You ridin?" Sin noticed how talkative Elan was so he figured he'd ride and smoke with the lil homie to soak up info on how the streets had been lately.

"You smoke . . . Roll up." Sin said tossing Elan a bag of haze.

"What you on out here?"

"Not much . . . I just got out the county . . . I'm trying to get back forreal, fuckin with 1/2 ounces."

"Word!" Sin said as he glanced at Elan out the corner of his eye then lit the half smoked blunt he had in his ashtray. Sin didn't think his name was too hot in the streets right now cause he'd been in the studio for months but he still liked listening to the young boys cause just like scandalous hoes they gossiped. All they wanted was to ride, smoke and be seen with people like Sin, for that they'd be loyal in hopes of getting the help they needed to reach the next level. As Elan passed Sin the blunt he leaned back at the light feeling the haze in his lungs, then asked Sin

"Ain't you from the JL block?"

"Yea . . . Why?"

"Ain't nothing . . . I was getting on with Spank a while ago."

"Word . . . Who you getting out wit now?" Sin asked.

"Flick . . . you know him . . . Him and Monster got it on lock in the hood." Elan said as he went on. "I don't fuck with them forreal, just if I can't find none of my ni$$az I'll call one of them."

"Yea I know who they is . . . But I don't know them personally" Sin said lying. Sin had knew Flick and Monster for a long time and had even terrorized their crew in the past.

"Damn bra . . . It's been a couple years since I seen or heard bout you . . ." Elan began but his words trailed off. It was obvious Elan couldn't conceal his thoughts, it was written all over his face that he knew something bad. Sin hoped it was about Flick and Monster cause he knew they were Kent's people and unsure if they suspected him in Kent's disappearance or if they wanted beef with Sin. Sin knew he had played his cards right by not acknowledging how well he knew Flick and Monster or sounding too anxious to hear about them.

"So what's on ya mind lil homie" Sin asked passing the blunt back.

"I remember where I just heard your name bra . . . But you ain't hear this from me." Elan said getting serious.

"Ok" I was over this bitch name Talacie's house in the hood and I heard Monster and Flick arguing about testify'n on you or talking to some detective about you . . . Something like that bra."

"I don't know but it was some police shit bra . . . They say you been try'n to rob and extort ni$$az . . . Said a ni$$a should've been got at you." Sin sat for a minute in silence but when he did speak Elan could sense the anger in his tone and see the destruction in his eyes.

"That's peace that you kept it one hunit with me on that . . . Stay away from them snitches lil homie . . . They'll receive their justice in due time." Sin told Elan in a calm voice that had Elan confused and wondering why Sin wasn't screaming how he was gonna kill them.

"Where you try'n to go?" Sin asked Elan.

"Shit drop me off at the 7-11 up here so I can grind this little pack." As Elan went to get out Sin handed him the $5000 he was gonna gamble with and told him to "stay sucka free" before he pulled off with murder on his mind . . .

Chapter 8

Born Cipher was in Lucasville on a felonious assault case so Sin had to figure out another route to take in order to get these snitch ass cowards before he even caught an indictment. Touching the screen on his IPhone Sin called his cousin Spank knowing he'd either handle it or have someone handle it. Also wanting to check the lil homie Elan's creditability since he said he used to buy work off him.

"What up cutty." Spank answered after two rings.

"Peace God, how you rockin?" Sin asked

"Come on man don't start that Godbody shit." Spank said as he took a deep inhale. Spank was two years younger than Sin, born on the same day to Sin's mother's sister so they had always been like brother's. Spank was as street as it got and wasn't ready to change. So although Sin respected his mind he always shot jewels and food for thought his way to make him think deeper. Sin was the first 5%er in his family but he never tried to force his way of life on his fam, he knew they'd come around eventually. So far only Ason had started studying.

"So what it do cutty, I'm in Ohio and we need to get together A-Sap or I may be doing a L-Bow." Sin told Spank with all seriousness.

"Damn cutty. Meet me on the JL in about an hour and we gone build, as you'd say." Spank said using some 5% lingo.

Sin hit the highway after calling his baby mother Kia and telling her he'd be back up in a few days. Sin was doing 92 mph down I-75 mad as hell and racking his brain to try and figure out how these hoes was gonna try to hit him with these bodies. He knew all the evidence was hear say, nothing physical at all but the way these crooked ass detective's worked, he figured they had these cowards lying as if they witnessed something. Little did they know Sin's ears stayed to the street and for his life he'd definitely bust his heat . . .

Sin and Spank came up with a master plan to put these snitch ass ni$$az where they belonged, in the dirt. So Sin was feeling a bit more relaxed. Looking down at his phone book section he tapped the screen to pull it up, already knowing who he was bout to call but unsure of the number Sin scrolled down to "PYT" and hit the call now button. Sin's PYT was a slim brown 18 year old he'd met a few month's after his release name Meagon. He wasn't too much into younger chicks but for some reason he liked fucking with a woman who didn't know all his past player episodes. After 3 long rings Meagon answered with a innocent sounding "Hello".

"Finally, there's that sweet voice I been missing." Sin said knowing he'd already made her smile.

"Well you could hear this voice everyday if you'd quit changing your number." Meagon told Sin before asking him, "When can I see you?"

"Well I was hoping you'd spend a few days with me, how does Gatlinburg, Tennessee sound?" Sin asked already knowing she'd be with it.

"Of course I'll spend time with you, let me know when so I can pack a bag". Meagon started to go on before Sin cut her off.

"Nah ma, you don't need no bag, just be dressed by 9:00am tomorrow we'll get clothes when we get there."

Meagon was ecstatic when they hung up and looking forward to going out of town with Sin but not as much as Sin was to be lining up his perfect alibi for the shit Spank was about to do. Two days later Sin and Meagon were leaving a shopping center on the Main strip when Sin got a call from Spank saying.

"You good cutty, breathe easy and get at me when you come back."

"It's on cutty, I love you," was all Sin said in response before hanging up and throwing the burn out phone he'd had just for that call into a sewer. Unable to hide his happiness Sin told Meagon he wanted to call it a night then pulled her close and whispered in her ear his intentions for the rest of the night. Smiling ear to ear Meagon grabbed Sin's hand and pulled him towards the car. As soon as they entered the room Meagon sat Sin down and started to do a sexy little strip tease. Sin snatched off his shirt and leaned back as Meagon continued till she was standing in front of Sin in just her boycut panties. Sin leaned up and snatched off his jeans shorts and boxers in one try as Meagon seductively walked towards him reaching for his semi hard dick. Meagon stroked Sin as she leaned down to take his bellhead into her warm mouth. Sin loved how her lips seemed to fit perfectly around his dick every time she gave him head. Meagon started to bob up and down which got Sin rock hard and placed him on the verge of busting a 30 second nut so he sat up and told Meagon to lay down on the bed. Sin started sucking Meagon's titties hungrily, spending long moments on each one. Meagon's titties weren't that big, just an handful but her skin felt so warm and soft under his lips that by time he moved down to her pussy he was feeling festive. Meagon's pussy was like a 5 star dining restaurant and Sin dove right in face first, licking up all the juices that lingered between her lips. Meagon started to moan and lifted her hips towards Sin's face so Sin sucked on her clit and slid 2 fingers inside her pussy. Meagon's moans grew louder as Sin began stroking her G-Spot while licking her clit as fast as possible. Knowing she was on the verge Sin pulled his fingers in and out of her pussy just as fast as he licked her now rock hard clit. Meagon exploded in climax all over Sin's face and hand as he tried to continue she pushed his head away and told Sin.

"Fuck me baby I need to feel you deep inside of me." Not needing to be told twice Sin stood up and flipped Meagon over roughly placing her face in the mattress and her ass in the air, Sin grabbed a condom Meagon had brought with her and put it on and entered Meagon's pussy in one swift motion going till he hit the back of her walls. As Sin began stroking he grabbed Meagon's waist to prevent her from crawling away.

"You like this dick don't you Meagon, yeah you love this dick." Sin said as he continued to fuck Meagon hard and fast just how she liked it. Meagon attempted to throw her ass back but every time Sin hit the bottom of her pussy hole her knees buckled. Feeling his nut bout to cum, Sin stroked harder as Meagon kept throwing it back. Sin shot off his nut triggering Meagon's own climax and coating his dick causing it to slip it out. Looking down Sin seen a puddle of wetness on the bed and laughed to himself. Meagon had laid forward, exhausted after her orgasm's, she layed there elated for half an hour hoping to be pregnant. Sin took a shower still happy as a kid on Christmas Day at the news he received earlier.

Chapter 9

Leaving his office at the 5th precinct Det. Hicks ran into Det. Williams. "How's it going partner?" Hicks asked as Williams stopped in front of him.

"Hope your not planning on filing any of that paperwork anytime soon." Williams said looking over the large amount of papers Hicks held.

"Yea . . . Why not?

"Need a few more detectives on the north side for a shooting."

"Well that's gonna have to wait . . . I've got two witness statements for the Mallory Court murder 3 years ago and I am headed to the prosecutor's office to start the warrant and indictment process."

"A 3 year old murder." Williams laughed.

"This here is an 1 hour old double murder . . . So put that shit on your desk and come on . . ."

Thirty minutes later Det. Williams pulled up to the crime scene. From the front of the house there appeared not to be a crime scene, just a well kept 2 story brick house in a quite area north of Dayton. As Det. Williams processed the front for clues, Det. Hicks was lead around back of the brick house.

"This must've been what they call their stash house." Det. Harris a short fat balding white guy with thick glasses said to Hicks.

"From the looks of it, the suspect just pulled up next to the vic's and unloaded, driver probably hit first and passenger second. He was a couple yards away from the vehicle apparently try'n to get away."

"Any identification?" Hicks asked as they entered the driveway in front of the garage where he seen the passenger laying face down with multiple shots to his back and one to his head.

"Were gonna have to wait for prints or dental records to identify the driver, he took 3 point blank to the face." Harris said. As the coroner approached Hicks turned his attention to the navy blue BMW, the passenger door was open and through it he seen what was left of a man's head scattered all over the dash.

"We're thinking the suspect followed the vic's or sat until they arrived." Harris was saying as the coroner flipped the body. Hicks eyes widened and his stomach dropped.

"Recognize the vic?" Det. Harris asked noticing the bewildered look on Hicks face.

"Yes . . . Fucking yes . . . Donald Wilson, aka Monster. He was my fucking key witness on a homicide I been working on for 3 years." Hicks jogged to the car to see if he could make out the other vic's identification but with no face it wasn't easy. Hicks almost knew for certain that this short guy was Flick . . . Charles Cummings. From a distance Williams noticed Hicks standing next to the BMW visibly upset about something. Williams made his way over to Hicks. "So what's got your panties in a bunch detective?" Williams asked Hicks.

"The fucking vic's are Donald Wilson and Charles Cummings."

"Ok . . . Is that suppose to ring a bell"

"Not to you, but they were my whole case." Hicks said walking back towards the front of the house where the dark green Crown Victoria they drove was parked. Williams who was about 6 inches taller than Hicks 5'8 height and darker than his brown complexion followed behind Hicks while digging in his pocket for his keys.

"Don't worry buddy we'll get whoever did this . . . After all they left the murder weapon." Williams told Hicks as they drove off towards downtown . . .

"So how do you know the vic's?" Williams asked halfway back to the precinct. Hicks had told Williams about the murder of a woman in Mallory Courts and he'd knew Flick and Monster knew something because the murder victim was their drug connections wife and he'd all of a sudden disappeared as well. It was known that he controlled the drug flow around here but they sold all the product for him and with him out the way they would be in charge of it all. Hicks explained how he put pressure on them and came to find out they had nothing to do with it but knew who did.

"So they wrote the statements and were willing to testify on this other guy?" Williams said cutting to the obvious.

"Pretty much . . . After a few threats. That's where I was headed before you came and fucked up my entire day."

"Well look on the bright side . . . You now have motive to charge this other guy with not 1 but 3 murders."

"Yes if I can establish that Wallace knew that these two were gonna testify . . . Not to mention I hadn't started the warrant process yet."

"Are you kidding me . . . Of course he knew . . . Word spreads throughout Dayton and Springfield . . .

It had been a few weeks since Spank had handle the situation for Sin and Sin was back to his comfortable shit. He'd fucked with Meagon a few more times and had even got her to pose naked in some pictures for him. He was on his way to drop the camera off to be developed before heading to the JL to kick it with Spank and give him twenty thousand for putting the murder game down.

As Sin pulled up on the JL he seen Spank, Geezy, and Larry Love all sitting on the porch. Sin jumped out his whip and greeted all of cousins in Peace before telling Spank he needed to holla at him in the house.

"What's good Cutty?" Spank asked as they entered the front room then the kitchen, the same kitchen where Sin had Nene and Missy whip up his work. It was hard to believe all that had transpired since then but Sin always understood that reality was what was real and what Spank had done for him was real as fuck.

"Damn Cutty what's up with you, you aight?" Spank asked taking Sin out of his daze.

"Yea yea fam I'm peace, I just wanted to drop this bread off to you" Sin told Spank as he pulled a stack of hundred dollar bills outta two separate packets. Spank knew by the size of each stack that they were ten thousand a piece, he knew money well. Stuffing the bills in his jeans he gave Sin a dap and hug before they went back out on the porch where Geezy and Larry Love were talking about the latest hoes they'd fucked. Sin and Spank jumped right in the conversation as if they'd been there from the start. All three took shots at Larry Love saying he hadn't had a bad bitch in years and all he could knock was the same old hood rats.

"You ain't fucked no bad bitch since your baby mama kick you out?" Spank said and laughed at his older brother.

"You sick as fuck, I just fucked Neisha the other night when she came over with Nivea" Larry Love replied defending himself.

"On the real I been on some chill shit fuckin with the studio so I ain't bagged nothing new lately" Sin said pulling the heat off Larry Love.

"Nah Naomi just got you scared to death." Geezy said and everybody laughed. "Me on the other hand I been running though hoes on campus and I got a new little chick down here name Meagon"

At the sound of Meagon's name Sin perked up and as Geezy continued he knew it was the same chick he called his P.Y.T.

Sin started to describe Meagon to Geezy with a smile on his face. "Son I just took that chick to Tennessee a few weeks ago and I been fucking or getting head in the Chevy on the regular." Sin told Geezy who was now laughing. This wasn't the first time they'd been fucking the same bitch so it was of no surprise to either of them. Sin got to telling Geezy about the naked pictures he just dropped off to be developed and was bout to explain how he had Meagon posing when Geezy got up and ran to his car.

"Peruse through these." Geezy told Sin as he handed him a digital camera. Sin couldn't do nothing but laugh as he seen Meagon spread eagle on the same bed he'd took his pictures of her on. Passing the camera around so all could see Sin and Geezy plotting to see if they could get Meagon to do a threesome. After all she was fuckin both of them already, why not do it at once. It didn't take long to formulate their plan and Geezy to call Meagon and start putting in motion. Sin stayed on the JL a few hours before he hit the highway headed to Dayton to pick up Infinity off the school bus.

Chapter 10

"Infinity laughed and ran into circles around the yard as Sin chased her.

"Come here . . . I got chu." Sin said as he scooped her up into his arms.

"Whose daddy's Understanding?"

"I am"

"Well give me a thousand kisses." Sin said as Infinity wrapped her arms around her daddy's neck and gave him uncountable kisses on his cheek. No matter how deep Sin had gotten into the streets he'd never disowned his responsibility as a father. He'd just gotten Infinity off the school bus and as usual he stayed to spend quality time with her and her mother Kia. They had never been a couple, she got pregnant the first time they had sex at 14 years old she was afraid to tell anyone, even Sin. At 8 months Sin finally learned he was gonna to be a father but was too scared to feel anything but nervousness'. Infinity lived with Sin and his mother for majority of her first 2 years so there was no time to stay nervous. Sin had to man up then and had been doing so ever since. Sin provided for his daughter and respected Kia for never having miscellaneous men around his seed, nobody but family had ever babysat. Kia had a nice condo with a balcony overlooking the fenced in front yard. The interior was decked out in black and white carpet and furniture, she had high rise ceilings and expensive looking picture's all the over the walls. Her condo sat back from the street and Sin loved the feel of privacy he got whenever he was over here. Infinity was 8 years old and dead on her mother and father who people constantly mistook for brother and sister when they were younger. Sin had met Kia at a high school basketball game in Springfield, he knew immediately she was from outta town so he got at her during the first half of the game. She had a gorgeous face but at 14 years old Sin liked how she seemed advanced in everything. She was a female version of him and he had to have her. Kia wasn't fast, actually she was a virgin when she met Sin, she was just more mature than her age . . .

"Your grilled chicken is ready." Kia said standing on the door step in a pair of Seven jeans that appeared to be painted on her frame. She had on a Educated Thug Misses wife beater top that was white with gray letters, her French manicure and pedicure were freshly done and her open toe scandals showed off her feet.

"I want some cereal mommy." Infinity said as she ran in the house. Sin was right behind her but slowed to a halt when his phone started to ring, the number was unfamiliar but he answered anyways.

"Peace" Sin . . . What's up?"

"I'm wit my daughter . . . Who is this?"

"Easha ni$$a . . . Don't act like you don't know me."

"Shorty, I don't know any Easha so how the fuck you get my number?" Sin asked signaling Kia to go into the house with Infinity.

"From your ni$$a . . . We all over here kickin it but anyways, you crazy. "Why you kill Flick and Monster?"

"What"

"Ni$$a you out here shuttin shit down." Easha said.

"Nah bitch . . . You talkin reckless . . . I don't know you or them names you throwin out . . . Don't call this fuckin phone no more." Sin said as he hung. Sin's mind was racing now and his heart was in his stomach. Sin knew Spank had handled the business right so how the fuck was his name out there in anything, the streets talk but this was fast.

By now Sin had sat on the front steps and Kia had come back to the front door.

"What's wrong?" She asked.

"Nothin ma." He said standing up and turning to face her. Kia could see worry in Sin's face so she said, "leave them streets alone and stay with your daughter tonight." Sin had business to handle in them streets, serious business that could make or break him but Kia's offer trumped all.

"Ok ma let me make a phone call to Spank real quick, and then I'll be in the house." Sin told Kia but noticed the change in her expression and sensed danger. Sin turned to see two unmarked police cars and one patrol car coming towards them, he knew what it was.

"Send a lawyer downtown . . . Don't answer no questions either."

"Sin I know." Kia cut Sin off as Infinity came to the door.

"Come here princess . . . Daddy need some love." Sin said as he hugged his daughter and cherished her embrace.

"Go finish your food." Kia said. Sin looked at her like she was stupid.

"I don't want her to see you cuffed up."

"You right." Sin said letting his princess go back in the house.

"Sincere Wallace . . . Mr. Wallace please put your hands where I can see them. One Det. demanded. Sin gave Kia a quick nod of understanding then told her to go inside.

Chapter 11

Over 3 years and 2 appeals denied later, Sin sat in his cell at Lebanon Correctional Institution. All the money he had stashed couldn't seem to free him of even 1 of the 3 life sentences he was handed upon conviction, he knew why though. This crooked ass system was withholding evidence. Sin was convicted on all circumstantial evidence, nothing physical and not one witness. The bitch Easha was just an C.I in a jam looking for a get out of jail free card when she made that call to Sin. The city was dirty but money couldn't clean this mess. Only a inside connect could help Sin now. The .44 Magnum Spank purposely left at the scene had prints on it but they weren't Sin's or Spank's. This should've lead to the investigation elsewhere but Hicks had it out for Sin, so he played the game raw . . . Sin cracked his window and lit up a joint of dro, his stash was low but he knew he'd be straight come second shift if his c/o bitch was working. She was from Dayton and had been on Sin's dick for about 8 months now so she kept Sin with a ounce of dro to smoke and at least 10 to 20 oxycotins to hustle every couple of months. Jazz came into the cell block at shift change, did her routine range check, then stopped at Sin's cell.

"Peace King."

"Peace ma . . . What's good?"

"Everything, step out so I can search your cell real fast." Jazz told Sin as she put on her rubber gloves. Sin stepped out and walked to the ice machine as Jazz dropped off his pack and rummaged around his books and clothes like the shake down was real. Removing the back off his radio she placed the pack where the batteries belonged, then exited his cell.

"So was everything there?" Jazz asked Sin standing at his door.

"Yes . . . I'm straight." Sin said tossing his mail on the bed.

"Why you looking so evil?"

Sin brushed off the question Jazz was asking and flipped it around on her.

"What's up with Adrienne? Sin asked

"I'ma keep it real Sin . . . I don't know how to ask her something like that . . . She could lose her job or even get locked up."

"She got access to the evidence room . . . She authorized personal right?"

"Yea . . . But only on request . . . That bitch don't even have her own keys." Jazz said

"That's irrelevant right now." Sin told her.

"Look take this list of evidence and have her mark down everything that's in there."

"How?"

"She'll find a way . . . If she see's anything not on this list have her copy down the numbers off of it . . . Especially the gun I know from the murder scene I know it's there.

"Why not have your lawyer subpoena it in a motion to suppress?" Jazz asked as if she knew how this shit worked.

"Think logically, if I know about the murder weapon, then I'm implicating myself."

"Oh"

"Ma you know I ain't gonna make no moves that don't add up so stop questioning my logic." Sin said as he turned to walk to the back of his cell aggravated with the situation.

"Ok baby . . . I'm sorry . . . I'll call her tonight to talk to her about it." Jazz said.

"Just hold me down ma." Sin said staring Jazz in her eyes. Sin knew all he needed was to prove they'd had a murder weapon with someone else's prints on then the whole time to show misconduct and give back these life sentences.

"You gotta help free your King so you can stand next to me as my Queen." Sin told Jazz as he walked towards her.

"I know baby . . . I been showing weakness and I'm sorry. No more of that . . . I need my King home to reclaim the throne." Jazz said as she winked her eye at Sin and walked off to pass out the rest of the mail . . .

Sin had been reading for a hour and a half or so when they called chow and rec but he had no intentions on going, he never went when Jazz worked his block. Getting up Sin started getting ready knowing in 10 minutes his door would pop open and Jazz would be waiting in the mop closet. When Sin entered the closet Jazz was there ready to get to it. They had been having these little rendezvous for the past 4 months so they had the timing down to the tee. In 15 minutes a rover c/o would come to the block to do a check . . . Sin pulled his dick out and watched Jazz wrap her luscious wet lips around it before giving him 5 long deep throats that had him ready to bust. Pulling back up his dick Jazz worked her suction on Sin's head causing him to bust his nut quickly. Sin could feel the cum being sucked outta him and his knees almost buckled. Jazz slowed her sucking and deep throated Sin again taking the last of his cum in the back of her throat.

"Ain't none left ma . . . Be easy before you get us knocked."

"Damn baby . . . I need you home." Jazz said squeezing her thighs together in an attempt to soothe the throbbing she felt in her walls.

"I need you to beat this pussy up."

"I got you next time you work ma." Sin told Jazz as he pulled up his sweat pants.

"I'll let you know what's up with Adrienne in a few days too . . . K?"

"That's peace ma." Sin responded then watched Jazz walk to the c/o's desk to prepare for the rover c/o to come in . . .

Sin sat on his bed and flipped thru his mail, he had a letter from Naomi and Ason as usual but the card from Cat was a surprise. He hadn't heard from her his entire bid, although Seven had wrote from time to time Cat never had. Tearing open the card Sin went on to read that she was sorry for not getting at him sooner and how she'd had a baby girl by some older dude who was jealous of the way Seven spoke of Sin. She explained how Seven had just got locked up in a juvenile prison and had to do 4 years. Sin was sick that Seven was going to have to go thru all the bullshit that come with doing time. Seven was only 15 years old if Sin remembered correctly. Cat put her phone number in the card so Sin decided he'd call her one day.

After receiving the card Sin got up to go take a quick shower, he had 30 minutes to spare till he had to call Naomi. Every few days he'd call at 3:15 to catch Asia getting out of school cause when he called at night him and Naomi talked the entire call. Naomi and Sin had a good relationship; they were the best of friends and parents. Sin told Naomi she'd always have his heart and he'd always have her back and she believed and respected that but she didn't wanna be more than what they were now. Sin respected her mind and besides he was doing a life sentence, he'd be selfish to ask her or anyone else to be more than a friend. Naomi didn't answer Sin's call so he called Sunday to check on her and Mecca.

Mecca had been born like 6 weeks prior to Sin's arrest, he was 3 years old now and reminded Sin of a young Ason. He resembled Sin a little, as well as Sunday, but he was a replica of Ason at that age. Although Sunday had a boyfriend she still rode with Sin in his darkest hour. She'd visit twice a month bringing Mecca once and coming solo once. She knew it was hard for Sin to raise his son from a visiting room but she admired how hard he tried. Sin and Sunday talked for two calls which equaled 30 minutes. It was close to 4 o'clock count now so Sin headed to his room to read the rest of his mail and put a build down on the days mathematics which was Build/Destroy!

<u>What makes Rain, Hail, Snow and Earthquakes and how it's symbolic to a relationship.</u>

The Earth is approximately covered under water ¾ of its surface. The Sun &Moon have attracting powers on our planet while its making the terrific speed of 1,037 1/3 miles per hour on its way around the sun. The Sun draws this water up into the Earth's rotation (which is called Gravitation) into a fine mist that the naked eye can hardly detect, but as this mist ascends higher and increases with other mist of water in different currents of the atmosphere until it becomes heavier than Gravitation, then it distills back to the Earth in forms of drops of water or drops of ice which depends on how heavy the mist was in the current of air it was in. There are some layers or currents of air that are real cold and warm and some very swift and changeable, so when the water strikes one of the cold current it becomes solid ice in small round drops in form, or in a light fluffy form which is snow, but this water is never drawn above six miles from the Earth's surface by the Sun and Moon. The reason it rains back on our planet is because the water cannot get out of the Earth's atmosphere with its high speed of rotating around the Sun. That makes this impossible! Earthquakes are caused by the Son of Man experimenting with high explosives. In fact, all the above is caused by man.

First off, knowing that the Sun and Moon/Earth are symbolic to Man and Woman, we can conceptualize how Rain, Hail, Snow and Earthquakes mirror our attitudes or emotions.

As a man I'm symbolic to the Sun so my attracting powers need to be knowledge'd cause I'm gonna draw water from my woman who is symbolic to the Earth, whether I choose to or not, its my nature to have these attracting powers.

My level of intelligence will determine whether it Rains, Hails, Snows or Earthquakes on my Earth(Woman). Water is the substance of Earthly life so Rain brings about positive growth in a relationship, but your attitude determines how often it Rains. Hail is dangerous and only manifest when the water I've drawn up from my Earth reaches me in a state of Anger, thus when the water goes to distill back to my Earth it causes her hurt. Her ability to deal with this Hail depends on the light I've been shining on her, cause she's the manifestation of my knowledge. When my light hasn't been shining bright that Hail could remain frozen at 32 degrees below or turn to Snow. If my light stops shining then it could cause Earthquakes, this is the destruction of a relationship cause it damages the foundation, destroying what was built. The goal is to remain divine, meaning pure and refined in my thoughts so as to avoid attitudes that bring about anything harsher then Rain back to my Earth(Woman). This is reality and is caused by the Son of Man, Who is the Son of Man . . . Me . . . , You!

Chapter 12

Adrienne sat behind her desk debating on making a call to Jazz. Her and Jazz had slept together three times. She knew Jazz had tried to resist her attraction to Adrienne at first but her body had given in. Jazz insisted all three times that she was still strictly dickly but Adrienne knew better, she'd long ago come to terms with the truth. "I'm a freak . . . Unlike Jazz . . . I like ni$$az and bitches," she'd tell herself. She didn't mind if Jazz was confused or not. Adrienne's cell phone ringing interrupting her thoughts.

"Hello" she said into the phone.

"What's up girl?"

"Shit . . . Waiting to get off." "Um . . . what you doing tonight?" Jazz asked.

"Nothing . . . Why?"

"I need to talk to you . . . Meet me at 8 Ball &Wings."

"Bitch . . . I'm tired and broke." Adrienne said smacking her lips.

"Drinks on me . . . Just be there . . . I need a drink bad."

"What's up something wrong?"

"Nah . . . We'll talk about it tonight." Jazz said.

"Ok . . . I'll see you around 11:00pm . . . Bye."

"Bye bitch." Jazz said then hung up wondering how to ask Adrienne to help Sin . . .

Just as Adrienne hung up Det. Williams stopped at her desk. He'd been shooting his shot at Adrienne since they'd first met a year ago but she wasn't feeling him at all. He had the look but no swag at all and his every move seemed timed. He was dark skinned, tall and muscular but all in all he was also a cop and her family wouldn't sit well with that.

"How you doing today?" Williams asked.

"I'm fine and you?"

"I'm ok . . . But could be a lot better if I had a beautiful woman like you on my arm at the movies tonight."

"I'm flattered . . . I really am but my close friend needs me for moral support tonight. After work I'll be meeting her." Adrienne told Williams.

Just as he was about to respond his Nextel chirped.

"Ok . . . Rain check?"

"Rain check." Adrienne agreed.

As Williams walked away she began to wonder if she should give him a chance, see what he was working with . . .

Adrienne sat at the bar with a shot of Hennessy watching the Grammy's. She'd only been there 15 minutes and already had declined two lames advances. Adrienne was a thick redbone with hazel eyes and a phat ass that ni$$az loved to stare at. She was about 165lbs but kept a flat stomach through her weekly workouts. Adrienne had sex appeal but heads constantly turned when Jazz entered a room. Tonight was no different as Jazz approached the bar in a Prada body suit that showed every curve of her body, including her pussy print. Ni$$az watched as these two bad bitches hugged and kissed.

"So what's up girl?" Adrienne asked.

"Let me get a double of Grey Goose please." Jazz yelled to the bartender. I need something in me first bitch . . . Wait till my drink come." She received her drink and took a sip feeling the burn . . . .

"I need your help girl." Jazz finally said

"With what?" Adrienne asked.

"Sin"

"How can I help him . . . What does he need my help with?" Adrienne said curious to know what was up.

Jazz took another sip before answering.

"Something in the evidence vault?" She said lightly.

It took a few seconds to sink in but when it did Adrienne said.

"Hello No . . . Bitch is you stupid . . . You want me to take something out that vault?"

Adrienne was going off but Jazz cut her off.

"No girl . . . Hear me out." She said feeling the liquid courage in her stomach.

"There's something, a gun that was used to kill the two people Sin's locked up for. It can clear his name and it's in that vault."

"And . . ."

"The prints on it aren't Sin's, the cops are withholding that information." Jazz explained.

"So why can't he have his lawyer ask for it through subpoena?" Adrienne said.

"Cause girl . . . In order for him to know the gun was there he'd have to have knowledge of the murder." Jazz said realizing how silly she must've sounded asking Sin the same question.

Adrienne sat in silence for a minute and Jazz ordered them another drink.

"So what exactly am I doing?"

"Just go in the vault and get this exhibit number or code number."

"Here" Jazz said smiling as she dug in her Prada hand bag for the list Sin had given her.

"Go through this list and when you find a .44 Magnum write down the exhibit number and description." Jazz explained.

"Bitch do I look like Inspector Gadget?" Adrienne said rolling her eyes.

"Whatever . . . You know what you doing bitch . . . Don't act all goody two shoes now."

"Yea . . . I got this . . . You ready to go?" Adrienne asked downing her shot of Hennessy . . .

A half hour later Jazz was in Adrienne's bedroom getting undress by her. Jazz pulled Adrienne close and began kissing her deeply, their tongues danced in each other's mouth's. Adrienne then took control like she always did and pushed Jazz up against the wall moving her kiss to her neck, then her titties. Continuing down she moved pass her belly button with her kisses until she had to get on her knees so her face was directly in front of Jazz's pussy. She threw one of Jazz's legs over her shoulder and started to run her tongue up and down her clit bringing it out its hiding place. Jazz started to squeeze her own titties and moan out "ooh . . . baby . . . fuuckk!" After only 5 minutes Jazz's legs began to shake as an orgasm flooded out of her pussy onto Adrienne's face.

Now laying on the bed Jazz watched Adrienne take off what was left of her lingerie in a sexy slow manner. Adrienne had been wearing a sheer bra and G-string set but the G-string was swallowed up by her phat ass booty. Adrienne layed on top of Jazz and kissed her deeply allowing her to taste the remaining juice from her own pussy. Getting excited Jazz flipped her over and reached to the night stand pulled out a 10 inch black dildo and rubbed it up and down Adrienne's pussy lips. After getting the dildo slick she pulled it back and licked Adrienne's pussy juices off of it.

"Put it in . . . Give it to me baby." Adrienne moaned and pulled her knees up to her chest. Jazz pushed the 10 inches deep into Adrienne's pussy.

"Ahh . . . Ah shit." She screamed as she came with the dildo about 8 inches deep in her pussy. What was usually sensual love making turned into raw fucking and sucking until they were both exhausted and fell asleep holding each other . . . The next morning Adrienne awoke first and hit the shower, dressed in a crème couture business suit that complimented her yellow skin tone and hazel eyes. She added a pair of 4 inch black Jimmy Choo's that were peep toe and a black patten leather belt to match her jet black hair.

"Morning baby." Jazz said as she rolled over and watched Adrienne put lip gloss on her lips in the mirror.

"Morning to you too . . . You was live last night girl."

"May have been that Grey Goose." Jazz said smiling.

"Yes I hear you . . . I'm off to work so I'll call you tonight and let you know what's up." Adrienne said and walked to the bed to give Jazz a kiss.

"You feeling good?" She asked Jazz.

"Uh huh . . . Do you think your gonna have enough access to the vault?"

"Be easy and don't trip girl . . . I got you." Adrienne said leaving the bedroom.

* * *

Adrienne was behind the desk at the property and evidence vault waiting for Det. Williams to show up as he usually did a few days a week. She had it all planned out, as soon as Det. Williams came in she'd flirt with him and gain entry through him. The rest would be played by opportunity although she figured it to be easier to get a picture of the evidence then to attempt to write anything down. She'd put this plan together this morning while choosing her outfit she knew she had to exploit her sex appeal to make Williams lose focus. She swore to herself that if she'd somehow got caught up, Jazz and Sin would take care of her $1500 a month luxury apartment, $600 a month lease on her BMW 5 series and whatever else she felt she was entitled to until she got a new job. Adrienne knew of Sin even before Jazz had started fucking with him. He had a name in the city that was well known and plus her brother's used to buy drugs off of him. Sin was one of the youngest ballers in Ohio and with all the ni$$az bitchin about what he took from them or their connects, everybody had heard something about him. Adrienne figured Sin still had a lot of money put up and strong connections to the streets because of the shit Jazz would tell her, from who still worked for Sin, to who'd give her money or packages to take him. All in all though from the way Sin looked out for Jazz, Adrienne knew if she came through for him while he was down, he would take care of her when he got out. A new car paid for and a couple thousand in the bank was all she needed but that was chump change to Sin and she knew it. The more she thought about it all this morning she knew she was gonna ride for Sin . . .

Det. Williams approached and interrupted her thought.

"Hi beautiful."

"What's up sexy." Adrienne replied paying attention to what his reaction would be. Det. Williams eyes lit up with surprise and his jaw slightly dropped. Her words were not anticipated but he try'd to carry on as if this was their regular greeting or as if he was smooth.

"So how's your friend?" He asked leaning on her desk. It took a minute for the question to set it, then Adrienne said.

"Oh . . . She's fine now . . . She actually just needed to stay with me all night."

"That's good."

"How thoughtful of you to remember."

"Well, I'm a good listener and very attentive." Williams said as he moved behind the desk to the vault door.

"Oh yea . . . I love that in a man." Adrienne said following him. Williams felt Adrienne's warm body press up against him as he stuck his key in the lock.

"So what's in there?" She whispered in his ear then let her tongue glide lightly across his earlobe. His nervous system failed him and all the smoothness left his body as he stuttered.

"Ol . . . old evidence."

"No privacy?" Adrienne ask seductively to give an idea that she was try'n to be alone with him. She could see he wasn't the aggressive type as they walked into the evidence vault so she knew she'd have to continue to tease and string him along in order to get what she needed. He'd been chasing her all year but now he seemed intimidated by her moves. As they entered the room she quickly took notice to the fact that everything was in alphabetical order so she needed to get him to the back by the W's for Wallace.

"Come over here sexy." She told Williams who obeyed like a puppy wanting a treat. Pushing him against the W shelves she told him to grab her ass so he wouldn't feel her pull her phone from her suit jacket pocket. After pulling out the phone she pressed titties to his chest and started to kiss his neck causing him to shake. Then she moved her tongue to his ear to get a better look at the box right in arms reach, luckily it said Giovanni Wallace. Pushing his head down to her chest she told him to suck her titties, knowing she'd be able to rummage through the box while he was down there.

Unbuttoning her jacket he quickly obliged and began kissing on her titties. Adrienne didn't know what a .44 Magnum looked like but when she felt a gun she prayed that it was the right one, then she pulled it out and photographed the label attached to it with the writing on it. Det. Williams was in a trans as he licked each nipple leisurely and squeezed Adrienne's 36C titties so he had heard nothing as his boss Det. McCoy entered the room.

"Detective . . . Detective." McCoy said sternly.

"Sir." Williams said jumping up from his feast on Adrienne's breast.

"May I have a minute with you?"

"Yes . . . Of course sir." Williams said.

Adrienne took that as her cue to get missing and she did just that as she hurried out the door to her desk where she quickly texted and emailed the picture to Jazz before she erased it and placed her phone in her purse. Through the door she could hear Det. McCoy yelling at Det. Williams about authorized personal only so she got up and went to the break room not wanting to be around when they exited the room . . .

Chapter 13

Three years after getting the evidence he needed Sin sat in his cell geeked up, but it wasn't from the dro he'd smoked. He'd got word that his conviction would be over turned in court on Thursday. After sitting in this cell for over 6 years he'd finally shook his triple life sentences on prosecution misconduct for withholding evidence that could have raised reasonable doubt. A 3 judge Federal panel had ruled in Sin's favor after his lawyer had filed a Post Conviction with ballistic's proof that the .44 Magnum had killed all three victims and the prints on the weapon weren't Sin's. The prints were actually Born Cipher's but he had the best alibi ever. He was incarcerated at the time of the double murder and nothing showed that he and the first victim knew each other to establish a motive. The Federal judge stated in their ruling that had this evidence been admitted at trial, Sin may not have been convicted. Today was Tuesday so Sin just had to make it till Thursday to hear the judge slam the gravel releasing him . . .

* * *

Meanwhile at the court house of Montgomery County, Judge M.T Hall and assistant prosecutor Linda Hobson were both angry and fearful of the backlash they'd receive due to the publicity this case would receive. The Bar Association could very well have her license soon and the judge would have to face the community who would most likely not re-elect him.

"Open discovery isn't the answer . . . Of course my office didn't provide Mr. Wallace with the evidence." She said to the judge while sitting across from him in his chambers.

"Well somebody needs to figure something out to put this fuckin animal back behind bars." The judge yelled.

"Yes sir, your honor . . . We're on it she said leaving his chambers. All of her years as assistant District Attorney and she still hadn't gained the respect or admiration she sought. As one of the few black women in the Montgomery County prosecutor's office, she'd had to work extra hard to gain any amount of success. But when she began to win everything changed, she began to receiving financial offers she couldn't refuse and once they had her in their trap they used, abused and disrespected her whenever they so chose. She'd sucked every white dick in that office as if she was a Mason's whore. She always felt and looked like shit but she'd do anything to keep her job and supposed high standings in the black community as a success. She was truly filthy though, selling young black lives to this corrupt system had never seemed to add up financially or morally. Her family hated her, she had little to no friends and she couldn't keep a man. Returning to her office she dialed the head detective at the 5th Precinct's number, he was the only other person who should've known about the murder weapon. On the second ring he answered . . .

"McCoy."

"Hi . . . Hobson here."

"Yes, I was expecting to hear from you and all I can say is time will reveal who it is and when I find what maggot under my supervision did this you'll damn sure hear about it. Now is there anything else I can help you with." McCoy asked Hobson.

"No, that just about sums it all up" Hobson said then heard McCoy hang up in her ear.

McCoy didn't need anybody pressing him about the Wallace case, especially some scared shitless prosecutor, he was pissed himself. Finally, their dirty laundry had been aired out. Hell the precinct reputation was far from squeaky clean but now somebody had taken shit to far. Someone was working for the Dayton Police but also working against them. McCoy called Hicks who was in charge of the Wallce case and 15 minutes later he was sitting across from him. Cuban cigar smoke filled the room as McCoy stared directly at Hicks.

"Talk to me . . . Tell me something." McCoy said.

"Look boss . . . I've questioned everybody who's anybody and it has to be someone with access to the evidence room . . . I'm thinking of just going down the list and investigating everyone individually." Hicks said to his boss. McCoy moved his mouse around then clicked a few keys causing about 20 detectives names and personal information to appear on the screen in alphabetical order. McCoy went down the list to see who he determined to be questionable when at the very bottom of the list sat Williams name.

"I haven't spoken to Williams yet but he was an investigator on the case with me." Hicks said as McCoy stared at the screen.

"Son of a bitch." McCoy burst out.

"Call this muthafucker."

"Who?" Hicks said confused.

"Williams that's who . . . Get that muthafucker in here now."

It hadn't dawned on him until he'd heard Williams name involved in the investigation. He wasn't sure but he had a hunch that the day he walked in on Williams and the attractive woman had to somehow be tied in with this. Hell it was the first and only lead they'd had, McCoy thought. Hicks called Williams and gave McCoy the phone.

"Hey loverboy . . . I want your ass in my office in the next 5 minutes or else." McCoy said and hung up before Williams could respond. Luckily Williams was still in the precinct's garage so he just returned to the elevator to head towards his boss's office . . .

"Boss you wanted to see me?" Williams asked poking his head into the doorway.

"Yea sit the fuck down . . . Your little girlfriend you was doing the oochie coochie with in the evidence room 3 years back is the reason Wallace has escaped three life sentences and my department is looking like a cess pool."

"Sir I don't understand . . . How is the possible?" Williams asked.

"You better find out that info . . . And quick! I want this problem solved . . . Do you hear me?"

"I . . . I . . ." Williams tried to explain but McCoy cut him off saying.

"I don't want this fucker to ever walk the streets of Dayton again."

"Yes . . . Yes sir" Williams said.

This couldn't be Williams thought, Adrienne used him to get information to free Wallace, if she had, then how he wandered. He'd have to do his homework to connect them and find out what he could about how she did it.

"So how was it?" McCoy asked.

"How was what sir?"

"The pussy . . . How was the pussy numb nuts." McCoy yelled.

"I . . . I don't know sir . . . We never hooked up after that day."

"What . . . Get the fuck outta my office asshole." McCoy said slamming his fist down on his desk. It was almost obvious that she was the culprit that leaked the information, now they had to figure out her motive. McCoy would drill Williams until he confirmed his suspicions and he'd then make Williams take care of this lady friend of his. McCoy wanted Williams to feel like an asshole for not seeing through a pretty face and phat ass. She'd never shown interest before and he wanted Williams to feel used so he could get him to seek revenge . . .

Chapter 14

Sin rode through the city in a triple black 2009 760 IE BMW with chrome 22 inch Asanti rims, listening to that B.G. "I gotta get back to the money." He stopped at every other corner store in the city and the hoe's, haters and spectators all watched as his doors opened and he jumped out in a black Educated Thug Wear Long John shirt, hard cut red monkey jeans all black, black New Era Yankee fitted cap and black construction Timberland boots to make his cipher complete. Sin had been wearing black everyday to represent for all his soldiers on lock down. He vowed to do this his whole first year home. With a 3 karat stud in his left ear and a 7 karat diamond tennis chain holding his universal Flag Pendant, Sin was still shinning regardless what color he wore.

"Peace." He spoke to the crowd of ni$$az and bitches as he passed to go in the store, driver door still open and ready to close by remote. Although he was in the hood Sin had no worries about somebody testing their luck and fucking with his whip. Sin brought a few blunt wraps and stepped back out the store, heads turned again and some noses rose but Sin ain't give a fuck. He had as many haters as he had muthafuckas who loved him. Only reason Sin hit the scene so hard was to make his presence felt, he had work to put in to get all the way back. Sin was still over the $250,000 mark when he left 6 years ago, but he was almost broke now due to all his lawyer fee's, house mortgages and other miscellaneous shit he'd still been paying out. Sin hustled in the joint but that kept him and Jazz comfortable and he'd given Adrienne $30,000 cash he made moving the oxycotins out of love for risking it all for his freedom. Damn there all of Sin's partner's from the JL were locked up so shit was far from glamour and glitz out here. His man's from Philly name Jim came down to link back up with him and shoot him some work. Jim wasn't really a hustler, he was a killer but while Sin was locked down he'd heard Jim had hit a Spanish kid in D.C for 10 bricks of heroin and hadn't looked back since. Sin knew he had to go extra hard now to get his money back right. Him and Naomi had agreed on a mutual split while he was down, so Sin knew he'd be in Ohio a while. Jim had business down here and Sin had linked him to the JL years ago and now he'd got with them and went all in to get that paper . . . Sin was meeting Jim tonight at "The Wet Spot" so he headed to Jazz's to get dressed . . . .

When Sin arrived Jazz was laying on top of her bed reading a sex novel in just her panties and wife beater.

"Peace ma . . . What you reading?" Sin asked heading towards the closet to undress.

"Peace King . . . It's an erotic novel." Jazz said looking up at Sin.

"Oh yea . . . So your pussy already wet then huh?" Sin said coming out the walking closet in nothing but his boxers.

"Uh huh . . . But not as wet as you always get me." Jazz said as she turned over and spread her legs to give Sin a view of her barely covered pussy.

Just as Sin started to walk towards the bed Adrienne walked into the room.

"Oh shit . . . My bad." Adrienne said backing out the room. Sin had never fucked Adrienne but he knew her and Jazz had been fucking around so he sat next to Jazz on the bed and told her to have Adrienne join them. Jazz knew Adrienne had wanted this but she always ignored her, now that Sin had spoke on it though she was with it. Jazz left the room and returned with Adrienne already naked, both of them were. Sin pulled off his boxers and leaned back on the bed. Adrienne reached first and started to stroke his dick, then they got into a sixty nine position and while they licked and suck each other. Jazz switched between them. Jazz spent time sucking Sin's balls, while Adrienne sucked his dick, then licking Adrienne's ass while Sin licked her pussy. After 15 minutes Sin busted deep in Adrienne's throat as she sucked up all his cum she let loose her own orgasm on Sin's face. Switching positions Jazz took Sin's dick in her mouth while she sat on Adrienne's face. When Sin was rock hard again Jazz stopped and told Adrienne to grab a condom so she could ride Sin's dick backwards. Adrienne did just that as she climbed up Sin's body and lowered her plump ass down on his dick. Sin slid in and her pussy gripped his dick instantly and she started cumming.

"Oh shit . . . Oh damn girl. Oh I'm cumming already." Adrienne told Jazz as she reached out and grabbed her titties.

"Lean back." Jazz told Adrienne as she lowered her face to lick on her clit while Sin's dick was still deep inside her pussy.

"Oh fuck . . . Oh my god . . . I'm bout to cum again." Adrienne yelled as she received the best sensations she'd ever felt. Lifting Adrienne up and flipping her over to face Jazz's pussy Sin told her to eat Jazz as he entered her wet pussy from behind. Adrienne obliged and began eating Jazz who came in a matter of minutes. Sin pulled his dick out of Adrienne's pussy and slid it into her ass causing her to lurch forward into Jazz.

"Oh fuck . . . I . . . I can't take it in there."

"Just relax ma. I'ma go slow." Sin told Adrienne.

"Yea baby . . . You'll love it once he starts his rhythm." Jazz told her.

Sin began slowly stroking Adrienne's ass but after 5 strokes he felt her begin to push her ass back up against him so he sped up and pounded her ass while grabbing her hips. Adrienne was no longer able to eat Jazz's pussy, her moans were louder and louder till she was out right screaming for Sin to beat up her asshole. Sin pounded Adrienne for 5 more minutes before he shot his nut off filling up the condom in her asshole. All three satisfied, they collapsed on the bed trying to catch their breath . . .

After an hour power nap, Sin got up to hit the shower, Jazz and Adrienne still laid there in a deep sleep so he tried not to disturb them. Dressed in some black Eviesal jeans with brown stitching, black Gucci loafers with gold pendant and a black Gucci sweater with gold G's all over it, Sin stepped to the mirror to grab his jewels from the lock box under it. Sin rocked the same jewel's from earlier adding a black diamond bracelet and black diamond studded Ice Tek watch.

"Can I go?" Jazz asked leaning up on her elbows.

"This a business meeting ma . . . I ain't fucking with the club forreal."

Sin glanced at Jazz's sexy ass sitting up next to Adrienne's thick ass who was still laying on her stomach from the long dicking Sin had put on her over an hour ago. Sin's phone rang and before he answered he seen it was Jim.

"Peace Sun." Yo so where you at?" Jim asked Sin.

"Just got fresh . . . We at the wet spot right?"

"Word Bond . . . I just wanted to tell you to have your whiz drop you off." Jim told Sin.

"That's Peace . . . She layin right here anyway."

"I'll see you in a few then God." Jim said before saying "Peace" and hanging up. Sin counted two $5,000 dollar stacks, put them in rubber bands and placed them into separate pockets before he told Jazz to throw something on so she could drop him off.

* * *

Twenty five minutes and 2 blunts of purple haze later, Sin was walking around the metal detectors and into the VIP to his table upstairs.

"Yo Ma, Ma get me another bottle of Rose Moet for my man's . . . Aight."

Jim said handing her $200 dollars. They dapped, hugged and sat back on the couch. Young Jeezy had the club rocking and from the top floor VIP Sin could see the sea of clubbers below him. He was above all and that's how he felt right now, on top. He'd beaten the odds of the streets, the corrupt system and their triple life sentence couldn't even hold him, nothing could.

"Don shell shocked." Jim said pointing at Sin who seemed to be in a trans.

"Nah, I'm peace sun . . . I just had a ménage with 2 of the baddest whiz's in the city fam . . . Now I'm here over looking all these people that belong below me. Every day I sat in that cell knowing I was gonna get back to the top and here I am God . . . On my way back to the top". Sin said grabbing the bottle of Rose Moet from the waitress.

"Well I'm glad you still feeling yourself God cause we got work to move." Jim said.

Sin was all for that and glad Jim was ready to hold him down. Taking a sip of his bottle Sin looked at Jim and pointed curiously at the waitress who hadn't left since giving Sin his bottle.

"Oh son . . . She come with the bottle." Jim said. Sin couldn't hide his grin.

"That's what's up . . . Don't go to far ma."

She was a tall thick drink water like a high yellow Tyra Banks but Sin knew he'd have to slide her the math and fuck with her another night cause like he told Jazz, "he wasn't fucking with the club forreal."

"So what you on God . . . That JL shit or you bout to hustle?" Jim asked Sin.

"Now Cipher . . . I'ma fuck with the north and east up here in Dayton this time . . . Just hustling.

I'ma let these bitches breath for now but once the team home ain't no telling what gon jump off."

Sin said knowing Jim was referring to robbing muthafuckas when he said JL shit.

"Word, word up I hear that, you gotta make it strictly about that paper. Eliminate as much of that hot shit from around you and get money son . . . Let the young'ns do the wild'n out. We can only get it if we out here yo."

"That's true in deed and believe me I'm so ready." Sin said smiling.

"Yo, you must've felt my vibes cause the north and east is all heroin . . . I got 2 bricks for you son . . . I wanna see you eat God on that young-fly-flashy shit you be on." Jim said tossing Sin the keys to a rental that had the 2 bricks tapped to the spare tire in the trunk.

"Good look . . . That's all I need to bubble up."

"I know son, that's why I'm holding you down . . . Just hit me with $180 son." Jim said before telling one of his goons to pass the dro. He handed one to Sin and lit one for his self . . .

2 Days later over Sunday's

"Sin . . . Get up, why you let me over sleep . . . You know I got class." Sunday screamed as she ran into the bathroom to take a shower.

"Damn." Sin mumbled to himself as he sat up and rubbed his face with both hands. He hadn't even meant to fall asleep, but he had.

"I need to start getting some proper rest." Sin told himself as he walked into the bathroom to take a piss.

"Ma . . . My bad . . . I ain't had no rest."

"Well, you ain't gonna get none today either. You gotta pick Mecca up from school." Sunday said turning off the shower and reaching for the towel Sin was holding for her.

"I get out of class at 8:00pm so if you need to, take Mecca to my mother's house."

"Nah. He cool with me . . . We gon hit the highway and go do some shopping." Sin told Sunday's back as she rushed off to get dressed . . .

Sin ended up picking Mecca up early from school, he hated picking him up at the regular time cause it was always like a class reunion from high school. Damn there every female he used to fuck had a child in some grade at this school. Mecca and Sin hit the highway headed to Columbus's Northern Light's section to fuck with his man's name Dwight who owned a clothing store name Hip Hop Culture. Sin and Dwight had been cool since 1996 when Sin used to spend thousands on Pure Playaz appeal in Dwight's first store. Dwight noticed the drive and determination in Sin through the question's he asked, so he began mentoring him about the business in 1998 . . .

"Peace to the God." Dwight said smiling as Sin and Mecca entered the store.

"Peace family . . . You see I bought the young God with me. You got some fresh threads for us or what?" Sin asked as he gave Dwight a pound and watched Mecca do the same.

"You know I got ya'll both some hot shit in the back . . . Come check it out." Dwight said leading the way to the back. "Plus we need to talk numbers God."

"I know fam . . . I know.' Sin replied nonchalantly knowing Dwight was speaking on the store he wanted Sin to hurry up and open. Sin had the intentions on opening up but he wanted to go hard on this music shit right now, plus he'd been fucking with clothes and stores since 2000. Shit it's 2011 now and time to move along, at least for a few years. Sin and Dwight had been building for a few hours until they came up with a number they both could agree on. Neither was trying to get over on the other, they had a lot of love and respect for each other and their way of life. Business was business though and they both possessed shrewd business minds. After handling business and building on the days mathematics, Sin told Dwight he'd be back at him next week. Grabbing his and Mecca's bags Sin headed to his whip to head east to a book store. Rare Books& Things was located on Livingtson Ave and ran by an older African couple that loved Sin. Sin had been ordering from them for almost three years now, ever since he'd seen their address in the back of a book he'd read while on lockdown . . . As soon as they entered the store Mecca ran up to Mrs. Mekebe and gave her a hug, he loved coming here cause he knew she'd have some kind of gift for him. Mrs. Mekebe had a way of sensing the good in people and had done that with Sin from the very first time he wrote to her to place an order. Mrs. Mekebe had seen beyond that address that showed Sin as an inmate and detected the intelligence of his words and the drive in him to become a better man. Once Sin had become a regular, Mrs. Mekebe made sure to order any new literature on or written by Five Percenter's. she respected Sin's way of life and they always spoke on the similarities between her African beliefs and Sin's Five Percent way of life.

"Peace and blessings to you queen." Sin said as he approached Mrs. Mekebe.

How's everything going with you . . . Are you staying out of trouble?" Mrs. Mekebe asked as she looked at Sin while hugging Mecca.

"I'm trying Mrs. Mekebe." Sin said shaking his head. "For the most part all is Peace in my universe . . . Have you received that new "How to Hustle and Win" book yet?" Sin asked looking over the counter full of incense.

"Yes we've had it a few days now . . . I was gonna call you had you not came in by this weekend. Hold on let me get it." Mrs. Mekebe said disappearing to the back. Upon her return to no one's surprise she also had a necklace for Mecca. Sin paid for the book, thanked Mrs. Mekebe and hit the highway headed back to Springfield . . . It was close to 7:00pm by the time he got back to Sunday's apartment. Mecca was knocked out in the backseat so Sin just carried him to his bed in Sunday's room. Sin knew Sunday was gonna be pissed he hadn't bathed him but he was tired. He intended to leave once Sunday got home but his body wouldn't allow it and he ended up sleeping through the night on Sunday' s couch . . .

Sin looked at the screen on his Iphone and seen it was his physical brother calling. "Peace to the God." Sin greeted Azon after listening to the operator and pressing zero to accept the call. "How you been lately bra, you ain't got at me in a minute." Sin said after Azon had returned his greeting of Peace. "Lil bra I been stressing, you know I'm bout to come home so I'm tryin to get my money right." Azon told Sin sounding weary. "Listen God stop stressin, I'm out here God so ain't shit to worry about. Get back in your 120's and focus on mind elevation, fuck some money, everybody got money! Do the math God." Sin told Azon in an irritated tone. "Fuck you mean quit stressin?" Azon said ready to go into a rant but Sin cut him off. "Today's math is Equality which is to be equal in all aspects. Build on that and you'll see why I say stop stressin." Sin said calmly. "Lil bra I do build I was in a cipher earlier building on the 6th Dimension and how it has no knowledge of itself." Azon started. "True indeed, their things that think their other than what why they are, they're nonexistent mentally." Sin replied then continued, "So why does the devil keep our people illiterate?" Sin asked Azon "So that he can use them for a tool and a slave. He keeps them blind to themselves so that he can master them. Illiterate means ignorant." Azon answered Sin's question quickly reciting the 6th degree of the Lost Found Muslim Lesson # 1. "Ok God now look at how the devil keeps our people illiterate. They say money is the root to all evil right? Well money is the main way our people are blinded, the devil has the money and has us chasing it recklessly; we stay ignorant to all the shit we do to obtain that money. Don't get me wrong God I'm a victim to the same perils as you but thru K.O.S(Knowledge of Self) we gotta continue to elevate our mental so we no longer gotta do devilishment for our money or be slaves to the devil's society." Sin told Azon in a tone that manifested his name of Sincere.

"I feel you lil bra, this time almost up. We hit the market in a few days so hold me down." Azon said as the operator announced 10 seconds remaining on the call. They both said "Peace God" and "I love you" then hung up. Sin immediately called Jazz and told her to get on the internet and put $150 on Azon books so he wouldn't miss the store. Sin knew how it felt to miss the store in their due to people not holdin him down but he always stayed straight due to Jazz or some other hustle he had jumping. Still he'd had a rough 6 years in and out the hole over drug investigations or 5% affiliation and he didn't want Azon to have a bid that way. He'd be out in 8 months and Sin had big plans for them together as a team. Legit plans! As soon as Sin flipped the 2 bricks Jim had fronted him a few days ago, he was getting out the game. Sin figured it would take 2 months tops but by the time his older brother got home he'd be done hustling work . . .

Chapter 15

Det. Williams had been trailing Adrienne for 2 weeks and still hadn't been able to connect her to Wallace. After noticing Adrienne visiting an unknown address frequently Williams decided to run a check on the address. Jazzmyn Litzy was the name on the house so Williams ran a check on her, Jazzmyn Litzy was an employee of the state so her photo, as well as place of employment came up. Williams didn't to much recognize her face but her job was very interesting, she was a corrections officer. Williams body grew hot with anger as he began to realize what must've happened, "they all three were linked together, Ms. Litzy, Adrienne, and that fuck Wallace," Williams thought to himself. Williams double check to be sure Ms. Litzy worked at the prison where Mr. Wallace had been housed, it matched and Williams blood began to boil. He phoned McCoy to explain what he'd just learned, when he did McCoy simply said

"I want Wallace dead."

"Ok sir." And this Adrienne lady . . .

"I want her out of my hair too . . . She better never step foot in my precinct again."

"But sir what do." Williams began but McCoy cut him off saying, "I don't care how you do it but it better get done. Do I make myself clear?"

"Yes sir." Williams said turning the key in his ignition to leave, just then he noticed Adrienne's BMW about to pull into her driveway. For the past few days he'd sit outside Adrienne's house in between trailing Sin around town, he went back and forth on if he should just blow her head off or not. He had a weakness for her though and even after finding out that she played a part in freeing a convicted killer and managed to make him look like a fool in the process, he still didn't think he could kill her. He jumped out of his car with his gun drawn and ran up on her quietly, she didn't see him until he was a foot or two away. Adrienne jumped showing that she was afraid but still managed to play it cool.

"Hey . . . Hey there how are . . ." She began.

"Bam" He smacked her across the face with his service revolver dropping her to one knee. Williams yanked her by the little bit of hair she had so she'd be looking up to his face, then told her.

"Get the hell outta town if you wanna live."

Then smacked the butt of his gun into the bridge of her nose causing her to lose sight then consciousness altogether. Williams jumped in his car and sped off to go continue his tail of Sin . . .

Sin rode thru almost every hood getting it in and hustling hard. He had two young goon's from his block putting in the delivery part so he just rode around collecting when the time came. Other than whipping up the work Sin wasn't to much handling the dope. He knew these crooked ass cops would be watching his every move and trying to put him back behind bars so he never visited the trap houses where the heroin was sold at. Sin didn't even smoke while riding around cause he didn't wanna give these pigs no probable cause to search his whip during a traffic stop. They had been following him around in unmarked cruiser's on the daily for 2 weeks now but he always noticed and stayed clean on them days. Today was a dark skinned muthafucka that Sin had noticed from a few other days but he was a clown and did a poor job of disguising his tail. Sin could tell he was emotional by the look on his face whenever he got caught at a light. I know these bitches don't think they gone scare me off. This my muthafuckin city Sin thought to himself as his phone vibrated on his hip

"Peace"

"Sin . . . You need to get to the house . . . They just beat Adrienne bad."

"What . . . What the fuck you talking bout." Sin said cutting off Jazz as she spoke over her tears.

"The police Sin . . . A detective . . . I don't know . . ."

"Put Adrienne on the phone." Sin said as he looked in his rear view to see where the cop was.

"Yes" Adrienne said in a whisper.

"You alright baby girl?"

"Um hmm." She replied but Sin could hear the pain in her voice.

Damn, what the fuck was these police on he thought to his self.

"You said the police did this to you . . . Tell me what happened."

"Yes, I was getting out of my car at my apartment and Det. Williams walked up behind me and hit me in the face with his gun . . ." She broke down then regained her composure to tell the rest of the story.

"So he told you to move out of town?" Sin asked in concern while paying closer attention to the Det. following him as they waited on the red light.

"If I want to live." Adrienne replied.

"What did he look like . . . The detective?"

"He's dark skinned, bald, a little taller than 6ft maybe?"

That was definitely the one following Sin right now he thought as he told Adrienne to put Jazz back on the phone.

"Sin be careful." Adrienne said.

"Don't worry ma, I'ma hold you down."

"Hello" Jazz said

"You and Adrienne go down to the JL . . . Take all that money over there with you and don't leave till I send somebody to follow you." Sin told Jazz as he kept watching the detective.

"Ok, but baby I'm scared . . . This the police you fuckin with."

"Look, don't worry bout shit . . . Draw up the 25th and 26th degree in the 1-36 . . . I'll call you back in a little bit."

"I love you." Jazz said, but Sin had already hung up . . . .

Hitting the speed dial Sin called Jim.

"Talk to me."

"Sun where you at?"

"In traffic . . . What's good?" Jim asked sensing the heat in Sin's tone of voice.

"This pig try'n to apply pressure on me sun . . . He just smacked up my whiz's girl with a burner and told her to move out the city if she wanna live."

"Yo . . . Yo slow down God. What you talking bout . . . Who Adrienne?"

"Yea." Sin answered then told Jim the whole story. Jim already knew the situation with Adrienne and how she'd helped prove the D.A was withholding evidence and basically set Sin free so he knew Sin was bout to ride for her like he'd do his own whiz.

"Yo . . . you hot Yo . . . We gotta get you out the city tonight."

"Nah, fuck that . . . These muthafuckas ain't gone do shit but follow me to the next spot. These muthafuckas following me right now sun."

"Ok son . . . So what we gonna do . . . I got the young goons on deck." Jim told Sin.

"They know what's up, they can't fuck with me . . . They did they homework, they know I'm Godbody/Hardbody so they try'n to play it foul. Now I gotta play their game and get at them before they get me." Sin ranted on. Sin had already thought of a plan to off this bitch ass pig that smacked up Adrienne.

"Sun send G-Code to the Food City out east and tell him to wear black jeans with a black hoodie." Sin said turning left on Gettysburg headed towards Food City.

"Tell G-Code to go in the store and wait for me." Sin instructed Jim.

Fifteen minutes later Sin had everything in place, he'd been wearing black jeans and a black hoodie also. He pulled up and double parked, running into the store where G-Code was already waiting. A minute or two later G-Code ran out, jumped in Sin's whip and took off with Williams following him. Sin came out and jumped in with Jim so they could follow Williams as he followed who he thought was Sin. Jim and Sin stayed a safe distance away careful not to alarm Williams.

"So what's next son . . . You gonna off him?" Jim asked.

"You already know. Today's math is Power Refinement and if not refined one's power becomes destructive . . . Only the true and living's qualified to serve justice and this crooked ass cop gotta pay for his ways and actions." Sin told Jim as he checked the clip on his p89 Rugar. He hit the dro hard 2 or 3 times, then passed it to Jim. Sin had a full clip in his Rugar that sat on his lap but he planned on empty'n it real soon. Jim made the call to G-Code informing him on where to park.

"Yo, make a left in Nickhales and once you get to that old building, park in the lot and jump out like you on the phone or something."

"Aight Yo . . . I got you . . . You sure you don't need me to squeeze off on this bitch ni$$a? G-Code asked.

"Nah son, I don't wanna take no chances just be easy we got this." Jim hung up and made the same left G-Code and Williams had made. Sin anxiously awaited and watched from the passenger seat ready to body this black devil ass cop. He'd never murdered anyone but he wasn't nervous at all . . .

The old building had 2 big dumpsters in the lot and a massive amount of trash that stood 9 and 10 feet high blocking the view in almost every direction making it a maze to enter and exit. Jim parked and Sin hopped out Rugar in hand and jogged to the 2nd dumpster where he peeked around. Williams was getting outta his car but G-Code acted as if he didn't notice. Just as the detective was going for his gun Sin raised his Rugar taking 5 steps towards Williams. Only 10 feet away Sin's aim was on point.

"Bang . . . Bang . . . Bang . . ." Sin let off 3 into the detectives back dropping him then putting 4 in his head as he lay on the pavement. As Sin ran back to Jim's whip he heard G-Code burn rubber.

"Yo, you good son."

"Yea . . . Hell yea pull off." Sin told Jim . . .

* * *

An hour and half later Sin sat on the front room on the JL where Jazz and Adrienne were. He knew shit would get real hot in the cities for him, and Jim had convinced him to lay low and build on a plan to get away, cause these dirty ass cops would kill Sin if they caught up to him. After a couple of shots of Grey Goose and his second blunt of purple haze, he had his mind set, he knew he had to leave Ohio for awhile.

"You ok baby?" Jazz asked walking into the room Sin was sitting in in silence.

"Yea I'm peace . . . Adrienne okay?"

"Yes, she asleep now." Jazz said and sat across from Sin in a butter soft leather sofa. Sin was laid back in a recliner with his feet up in the barely lit room. Beanie Siegel's "What cha life like" played low in the background and the words, "What cha know about solitary/locked down no commissary/and you wild already, had Sin vividly recalling all the days, months and years he'd sat in that lonely cell. Going back wasn't an option he thought as Jazz asked.

"So what's going to happen now?"

"I'ma disappear for awhile . . . You and Adrienne can stay here. I'ma leave ya'll some money so you'll be straight . . . . Just don't go back to Dayton or to your jobs." Sin knew Jazz wouldn't like them splitting up and seen her stand up to protest so he continued.

"Only other person know ya'll here is Jim so ya'll good . . . It's $100,000 in the floor safe in the closet."

"Where you going?" Jazz asked.

"I'll give you a number." Was all he could tell her. He hadn't decided yet and as he looked at Jazz's sexy silhouette he knew it would be hours more before he did. Sin put all the bullshit of today's events outta his mind and admired Jazz before telling her.

"Come over here sexy."

When Jazz reached Sin he already had his dick out for her to grasp. Once she did, she bent to her knees and sucked Sin to the verge of nutting before stopping and mounting his dick and riding him slowly till they cam and drifted off to sleep . . .

Chapter 16

In the next week Sin made mass calls to move his remaining work and by the end of the following week he was counting $180,000 cash. Still with 13 pounds of Dro weed and 1 brick of heroin, Sin made one last call to his partner Fat Shotty who moved heavy pounds of weed on the regular. He sold all 13lbs for $65,000, which he planned on leaving town with. Sin still owned Jim the $180,000 for the bricks of heroin so he squared that up before he got Nikki to do what she did best and drive. He'd known Nikki since elementary school and she had always been crazy about Sin. She'd do almost anything for him too. She wasn't street smart so Sin never had a position for her other than driving his money down south. He respected her so he never tried to fuck and had avoided her many advances for fear of losing her loyalty and trust. Sin loved her style, plus she was a certified dime piece, short yet thick, 5'4 150lbs with a ass rivaling Vida and titties to match. She also had a real pretty face and kept her hair short to show it off. Nikki was about her business in the Real Estate game. Down in Miami she owned a few properties along the beach. She knew how Sin lived and about the years he'd spent in prison but she didn't care about all that. She loved Sin cause he never disrespected her and always connected to her mental. There were plenty of times she was vulnerable and hurt but every time Sin was there to talk to and help her get through it. The place Nikki lived was a beach front condo, the size of two 3 story houses. It was decked out with a chandelier in the front foyer and white furniture in every room, setting the tone for a comfortable atmosphere equipped with 8 separate 55 inch plasma screens . . . Sin sat under a palm tree sipping on a Tropicana orange juice and smoking dro while Nikki typed on her laptop computer.

"Well, there's no warrant out for your arrest." Nikki said closing her laptop.

"Damn, that's good ma, but it also means these pigs out for blood." Sin told Nikki.

"Well their not gonna get it. You here with me and I'm glad you've decided to slow down out here Sincere." Nikki said looking in Sin's eyes.

"Me too mami . . . Me too." Sin said taking another pull on the dro.

"Baby I'm serious, I hate to see or hear about the thing's you've been through." Nikki said moving closer to lean up against Sin and look out at the beach.

"I could stay out here forever." Nikki whispered.

"Yea ma, that sounds like a plan huh." Sin replied.

"Um hmm and once I close the deal on the mansion in White Rine, I can sell my share of stock in the company so me and my man can get away." Nikki said in a matter of fact tone.

"Damn ma, I ain't know you had a man." Sin said turning to face Nikki.

"O, you fucker!" She said playfully punched Sin in the arm. Sin turned and began to play wrestle with Nikki in the sand.

"So I'm your man now huh?" Sin asked as he rolled on top of Nikki.

"Hell yeah you my man." She replied.

"Ma if I was your man we'd be fucking on this beach." Sin said looking Nikki in her eyes.

"Well we better get it poppin then papi." Nikki told Sin as she pulled him down on top of her. As the play turned into foreplay Sin and Nikki began kissing and sucking on every part of each others uncovered body parts. The sun was starting to set and the romantic atmosphere mixed with how long she'd wanted Sin, had Nikki's pussy soaking wet. Sin pulled down her thong bikini and removed her top to admire her beautiful 34DD titties. Pushing down his shorts Sin spread her legs wide and slid into her softly.

"Ahh." She moaned out and wrapped her arms around Sin's neck. Nikki threw one leg up and encouraged Sin to push deeper with her hip movements. Sin caught her signal and began to deep stroke Nikki; he then pulled her other leg up and began to speed up his pace.

"Auhh . . . Auhh . . . Ohh shit baby . . . Fuck me Fuck me papi." Nikki began to scream feeling her climax approaching. Sin continued to bang away at her pussy with both her legs up around his shoulders.

"Cum in me papi . . . Auhh yes, yes, yes papi fuck me like that." Nikki screamed then started speaking in Spanish while Sin fucked her good. Sin felt the bottom of her pussy every time he went deep and she let him know it by digging in his back, screaming, licking and sucking everywhere from his mouth to his ear and back. The connection they had was amazing for this to be their first sexual encounter.

"You cuming papi?" Nikki asked as she felt her own climax explode. Sin silenced Nikki by sticking his tongue down her throat as he gave her two last strokes then released his seed. Nikki felt Sin's release and screamed her pleasure into his mouth then wrapped her arms and legs around him tight, not letting go until his body was no longer tense.

Chapter 17

"Where the fuck is he?" McCoy yelled.

"Boss, I've had my guys raid every known drug house and put pressure on his known associates. We've questioned and threatened everyone but no one seems to know anything." Hicks told McCoy.

"Where's the girl?" McCoy asked.

"Well, nobody had turned and none of our guys have seen her so I'd assume she took our advice and left town." Hicks said.

"Family?" McCoy questioned knowing there had to be a way to get to Sin.

"Yes, an older brother who's currently incarcerated and a younger brother who seems to be clean. No record, college graduate and does a lot of work with the youth. Father unknown and mother moved out of town a few years back." Hick read off a sheet of paper. McCoy thought for a second if in fact Sin's little brother was walking a straight line then any tragedy would definitely bring him back. It's a cold game and McCoy would make Sincere come to him. An EYE for an EYE McCoy thought to himself, Sincere's brother for Williams. It had been 7 months since detective Ralph Williams was gunned down and McCoy knew Sin had done it. Now he'd obviously fled town thinking it would be all good. Now, his family would die off one at a time until he showed his ass. McCoy finished his thoughts and asked.

"So who's the younger brother?"

"Um . . . Donta Wallace sir."

"Ok, kill him." McCoy ordered.

"Yes sir, I'm on top of it boss." Hicks said leaving the office . . .

* * *

Coming into the police academy Hicks wasn't this corrupt, he'd cheated on his wife, smoke weed and stole money from young drug dealers but this was getting to be too much. He'd never had plans on setting up young black kids's from the same types of neighborhoods he'd grew up in nor killing one in cold blood. But it was to late to turn back now. He was connected to a team as filthy as the infamous LAPD of the 90's and to kill Sincere Wallace had become a priority so it was gonna be by any means necessary. Hicks knew he had to keep pretending to be one of them in order to survive. Under no circumstances could he go against the grain. Therefore Donta Wallace had to die. Not by his hand through, he'd planted a lot of drugs to put away innocent people but he'd never murdered anyone and had no plans of changing that, his conscience couldn't handle that. McCoy had continuously risen Hicks up in the ranks thinking he was heartless and knowing he'd do whatever the higher ups said to do. Hicks never questioned McCoy but this time he'd give the duty of pulling the trigger to another crooked detective under him.

The hit was carried out like a routine traffic stop, so when asked to step out of the car Donta showed no worry, knowing he'd done no wrong. As the two plan clothes cops questioned

Donta they brought up Sin's name causing a little worry to come into Donta's expression but not much. One cop stood in front of him badgering on and on about Sincere's whereabouts while the other moved around to the back of the car. Almost on cue the cop questioning Donta stepped to the side while the other raised his pistol and squeezed the trigger two times.

"Boom. Boom." The shoots echoed on the deserted street as they entered the back of Donta's head killing him before his body hit the pavement. Hicks sat silently watching it all from a safe distance as this young man casually dressed in designer slacks and button up shirt had just become a casualty of war. Donta was almost identical to Sincere despite their year age difference, but Hicks knew this would only be the beginning cause it wouldn't satisfy McCoy's thirst for Sin's blood to be spilt. Hicks wasn't as heartless as McCoy but he knew these Dayton city streets well and he needed the pay, not the payroll from the city but from the streets. McCoy had snitches, known drug dealers and out of town suppliers on a payroll. If they wanted to continue to sell dope they had to pay him and his detectives 15 to 20% of all profits weekly. Hicks had four mouths to feed so he was on his job constantly running for McCoy to collect their money. Picking up his cell phone Hicks called McCoy to relay the good news.

"Boss, everything's complete."

"Good, meet me after quit'n time at the Bar-N-Grill." McCoy said and hung up smiling . . .

Later that night Hicks sat across from McCoy with a well done streak and Corona in front of him.

"I'm guessing Mr. Wallace will be back in a day or two after hearing about his brother's death. I want word spread to all our men to terminate on site. I'll deal with the paperwork." McCoy told Hicks.

"Yes sir." Hicks replied taking a piece of steak into his mouth. McCoy reached into his blazer pocket and produced a yellow envelope then handed it to Hicks.

"This feels a lot thicker than usual." Hicks said curiously.

"Well, tonight wasn't the usual now was it?" McCoy said before sitting his jacket on the back of the chair and standing up.

"That's $35,000 . . . A $15,000 raise so let's go play some pool. Maybe I can win some of that money back. McCoy said walking to the back of the bar. Hicks couldn't argue with that so he took the last swig of his Corona and quickly followed his boss.

Chapter 18

The next day Sin and Nikki awoke around noon . . . In the 7 months since his relocation down to the bottom of the map Sin had been living it up in various clubs where he always had V.I.P status. No one in Miami knew Sin's story, the rich corporate white people all assumed he played some kinda sport. All the ladies he met thought he was a boxer and none of the hood ni$$a's knew him cause he had never sold a ounce of any drug in Miami. After doing all those years in prison Sin knew that's where the real non stop money was, so he devised a plan to keep several different prison's in Ohio flooded. He had solid soldiers from his hood in every prison b.u.t he decided to send a half ounce of heroin a month to the eight of them he knew could handle it. Sin had Born Cipher in Lucasville, Mandale in Warren, Junya in London, Hot Rod in Lebanon, Weezy in the Feds, Divine Melik in Ross, Mike B in DCI and Big Ills in Chilli. Sin made sure they all received a half ounce a month like clockwork whether it was through legal mail demo's, hoes smuggling balloons thru pussy or a c/o just bringing it to them. Regardless of how, it got done and after 7 months Sin had made close to $800,000 but only kept $392,000 for himself. The rest was all his partners profits and they all had their own spots they had him send their money. Everything was beautiful, Sin had 8 ounces left and planned to just flood all 8 of his partners with 1 a piece at one time and collect a $112,000 to put him over a half a million. Sin took about a hour getting the packs ready to be shipped to their separate locations before he got the call from his oldest daughter Infinity and her mother Kia. They were still in Dayton and Infinity had been acting up and throwing tantrums about not getting to see her daddy. Calming his daughter down, Sin told her he would have her come down to stay with him for a few weeks.

"Be good for your moms aight . . . We'll be together in a little while." Sin told Infinity.

"Ok daddy." She replied then gave her mother the phone.

"Hello . . . So what you staying down there for good now?" Kia asked curiously.

"Ma you know them dirty ass cops up there want my freedom. I can't stay up there no more but I ain't made up my mind as to where I wanna live yet." Sin told her.

"Well don't go no further than where you are now." Kia said.

"So what's up ya'll good, ya'll don't need shit do ya'll?" Sin asked.

"Um . . . Your daughter good but I could use some money." Kia told Sin.

"I'll send it Western Union in about an hour so have your cousin go pick it up." Sin told Kia knowing the police would be watching her. He always sent money to fake names and had one of her cousins pick it up using a code. No I.D required. Just then Sin's phone beeped cause someone else was calling in on the other line.

"Hold up ma." Sin said before looking at his screen to see who was calling. Sin seen it was his mother so he told Kia he'd call her back, then clicked over and greeted his mother with "Peace Mom."

"Sin . . . Donta's . . . Donta's." His mother said in between sniffs and tears.

"Yea mom . . . what's wrong?" Sin asked knowing the news couldn't be good due to his mothers tone.

"He's dead Sin . . . Somebody killed my baby." His mother cried.

When Sin heard that, his heart sank to his stomach. His lil brother was gone just like that. How, who, why? Sin couldn't think straight long enough to answer any of these questions. What he'd just heard wasn't adding up. Donta wasn't flashy so he ruled out robbery. Why was all he kept on wondering and through Knowledge of Self he understood he was the only one qualified to answer that question. After an hour of numbness Sin sat back and shed tears for his mother, his brother and whoever had done this cause revenge was a must. The rest of the night seemed like a blur as Sin rolled blunt after blunt and downed shot after shot to deal with the pain he felt. The weed and liquor couldn't cloud the truth that Sin was seeing clearly, he was the reason his lil brother was sent back to the essence of life.

"Damn I'm slippin." He thought out loud.

The tears had stopped a while ago because his emotions had went numb but deep down he was hurt bad. It hurt bad to know Donta's blood was on his hands. Nobody else knew cause Sin kept his business in the streets, in the streets where it belonged. Not his mother, children's mother's or his older brother who was still locked down till next month, knew half the shit Sin had been into. Jim was the only person who knew some of the shit Sin was on, so that was the first call after he'd sat on the dark porch in deep thought . . . Sin knew what these pigs wanted, they wanted his blood in the streets so they used Donta's blood to get to Sin's blood. Well it is what it is Sin thought listening to Jim's ring tone before he answered.

"Peace to the God . . . What it do scrap?"

"You catch the news?" Sin asked.

"Nah B . . . Why you on it or some shit." Jim said jokingly.

"Them pigs killed my lil brother sun." Sin said slowly.

"Son you . . . You serious?" Jim asked but Sin didn't even answer.

"When this happen son?" Jim continued questioning.

"They found him yesterday." Was all Sin said back.

Jim could tell it was about to get crazy. Sin was to calm about his brother's murder. Jim knew if anybody deserved to die Donta would be one of the last. The lil homie stayed off the streets and out the game. Even though Sin kept him with a nice stash, he still finished school, kept a 9-5 and did good shit around the community.

"Yo son, I been back in Philly for a few days to re-up but I'll cut this shit short and head back to Dayton tomorrow night. We can meet at my spot in Vandalia and then go from there." Jim told Sin.

"That's Peace, I'll . . ." Sin started but Jim cut him off and said.

"Son don't lose your head . . . These hoes gonna pay and that's my word.

Chapter 19

As McCoy and Hicks sat in his office. McCoy barked his orders.

"I want men on every corner . . . I want a positive I.D, then I want him followed until he's no longer endangering family, friends, or the public." McCoy said and received a head nod from Hicks before continuing, "the cleaner it looks the easier it is to clean up. I want this to look as if he was resisting arrest and went for a weapon . . . Am I understood?" McCoy asked finishing his speech.

"The funeral begins at noon but we assume he'll arrive early, in which time we'll be able to I.D, then follow him from there." Hicks informed his boss.

"Get your men in place." McCoy said dismissing Hicks from his office . . .

Detective Hicks had 4 undercover cops on hand to do the surveillance duty. They'd have no knowledge of the real mission or the reasoning behind it. All 4 were strategically placed far enough away not to have their cover blown. The funeral home was Dennis L. Porter it was on Yellow Springs St and ran right in the heart of the city. Next to the funeral home was a Hair

Salon called Shae's, in it Hicks had placed one of the cops. A Barbershop sat cata-corner across the street from the funeral home and had a cop placed there to watch the outside. Up the street across from Qualities corner store was a tire shop that one of the detectives parked at, while the 4th and final cop was to attend the service as if he was a old friend. By 10:30 all of Hicks men were in place and would radio to him the details of the day's events as he sat two miles up in Oasis Drive Thru's parking lot. The entire family had appeared to have arrived by 11:30 am but no Sincere Wallace was in site. The parking lot looked like a car show, all different paints, rims and models of new and old cars had pulled in to show their respects to Donta Wallace. Around 1:00pm all the flashy cars aligned behind a all white stretch limo full of Donta's family as it followed his pearl white casket being pulled by two beautiful horses. At the gravesite every color of roses was dropped along Donta's grave path as tears fell from all who'd loved and appreciated his life. One of Sin and Donta's best friends since childhood name JimiDaGoon had given the eulogy earlier and now was saying the final words as Donta was laid six feet underground. All of this had taken place without the presence of Sincere Wallace and upon hearing that Hicks slammed his radio to the floor of his cruiser . . .

* * *

Sin sat back in Jim's basement watching his younger brother's funeral on a Skycam surveillance he had installed in and around the funeral parlor. The trip to the burial site would be recorded on a camcorder for Sin to view privately later. He'd been fasting for 6 days and nights since he'd received the news of Donta's death and his mind was so clear and powerful that he knew he'd succeed in his revenge. Jim sat at his basement bar and watched Sin. He knew Sin was about to put a shrewd murder plot down on these pigs. He planned on being right along side of him too, making sure nothing went wrong. They'd already gone over every detail front to back on which detective's they'd kill. Sin figured it had to be Hicks cause he was the detective on the case that had him convicted in the beginning and he'd always been known to be a dirty cop. Besides detective Williams was already dead and McCoy was the one giving orders. Sin studied the entire history of his case's and of what the streets said about these two detective's, so he knew his war ended with McCoy. The entire situation had gotten to a personal level and for that Sin assumed that the orders were from McCoy attempting to avenge William's death. They wanted a war, so that's what Sin intended to give them. The first strike would be next week on Thanksgiving Day or what Sin liked to call Hell Day due to how the devilish pilgrims put their tricks down on the Indians to steal this land and make it a living hell. Standing up and walking towards the bar Sin said.

"The devils 6,000 year rule is over sun . . . Time to take these hoes off our planet."

"Yo I'm wit cha all the way son." Jim said and stood up to give Sin a pound and hug. They embraced like that for a minute or so before Sin headed upstairs to lay it down for the night, with murder on his mind . . .

It was a little past 9am and Sin was just finishing his work out. Sin stayed in excellent shape by lifting weights three times a week but since he wasn't around any weights he took it back to one of his penitentiary work outs and did 1000 Jumping Jacks, 1000 Squats, and 1000 Push Ups. Looking at his phone he seen a missed call from Azon so he sent him a text back telling him he'd get at him after he showered. Azon had been granted a release from the minimum security facility he was in, he only had 3 weeks left so after Sin paid his lawyer a few thousand to file the" extenuating circumstances motion" he was released. Sin had broke down and told Azon everything his first night out. Azon was crushed by Donta's death but he never blamed Sin and he wanted revenge just as Sin did. Sin had vehemently refused to let Azon be a part of the action; he justified it by saying someone had to watch over Mom. Reluctantly Azon agreed but he still continuously hounded Sin with ideas on how to pull off the revenge.

After showering Sin didn't call Azon right back, he had this quote stuck in his head and he needed to find out the origin of where he'd learned it. Sin flipped thru the "33 Strategies of War" but couldn't find the quote. Interrupted by his phone Sin sat the book down and answered "Peace."

"Peace lil bra. Why you ain't call me back yet?" Azon yelled at Sin.

"Cause I got this quote stuck in my head God, I'm try'n to find out where I know it from." Sin responded.

"Shit, if it don't got shit to do with this payback then its irrelevant." Azon said angry that Sin could think of anything else.

"What is it?" Azon continued.

"Warfare is the art of the deceit. Therefore, when able seem to be unable; When ready seem unable, When nearby seem far away; and When far away seem near." Sin quoted what had been stuck in his head all morning.

"Yeah yeah God, that's Sun Tzu in the Art of War." Azon told Sin.

They both had read that book, Sin had a few times but he didn't recall that part so he told himself he'd look it up later. Sin and Azon spoke awhile about Donta before Sin broke in to the day's Mathematics.

"Sun, today's math is Knowledge Born, all born back to knowledge which is self. Build in the alphabet." Sin told Azon. "The knowledge Born degree in the alphabet is S or Self/Saviour The blackmans knowledge of himself makes him a saviour of himself by borning or completing Self. Only you can save yourself." Azon said quoting the degree's.

Sin was pleased that his older brother knew and could speak the degree's. Azon hadn't reached the Lost Found Muslim Lesson # 2 yet but Sin still decided to build out of it to his brother. "The Knowledge Born degree of the 1-40's is: Q. If a civilized person does not perform his duty what must be done? Ans: If a civilized person does not perform his duty which is to teach civilization to others, he shall be punished with a severe punishment. Ezekiel 3:18 "When I say unto the wicked, thou shalt surely die: and thou givest him not warning, nor speaketh to warn the wicked from his wicked was to save his life: the same wicked man shall die in his iniquity: but his blood will I require at thine hand". St Luke 12:47 "And that servant which knew his lords will and prepare not himself, neither did according to his will shall be beaten with many stripes." Sin quoted.

"That's Peace God but how does it apply to hear and now?" Azon questioned.

"Well it's like this God." Sin said as he began to build on the question.

"In order to be civilized you must be qualified to teach the uncivilized, that's where Self/Saviour comes into play. How can you save someone else if you haven't saved yourself? You can't! We all receive severe punishments when we stray from being civilized and Donta's death is one of my severe punishments.

See God, I have knowledge of Self but I've still yet to master my lower self or carnal desires. I'm held responsible for the actions of uncivilized devils like Hicks, Williams, and McCoy. There's a such thing as duality in life God and the universe allows no debt to go unpaid, whether positive or negative. This war between crooked cops and hustler's in the inner city streets didn't start with me, its deeper than me God. This has been going on before our time. But I feel like Saladine who in 1184.a.d, took Jerusalem back from the devils after 199 years of war, they'd been at war 150 years before his birth. That's me God, and I give you my word that these devils gone pay for Donta's death." Sin told Azon meaning every word of it. "That's peace lil bra and I trust your word so I'ma let you handle shit." Azon told Sin as they prepared to hang up.

"I love you God, I'm out. Peace." Sin said then hung up.

After no sign of Sin at the funeral service's Hicks made a call to McCoy to inform his boss of the bad news.

"He didn't show up sir . . . He may be too afraid to return." Hicks said.

"Or he was there and your men were a bunch of fuckin idiots." McCoy responded showing his disapproval of what Hicks had said.

"Sir, I'm almost 100% sure he didn't attend." Hicks said as McCoy gave him a long pause and said nothing.

"I had men in and around the service sir, I even surveyed a bit myself. He just didn't show sir." Hicks explained.

"Tell you what, we'll give it a bit . . . Lay off of him for a while and see what happens. This is not over, it's far from over. We'll get Sincere Wallace." McCoy told Hicks as he hung up. McCoy was beginning to think that maybe Sin had went on the run with no intentions on returning . . .

Chapter 20

Jim sat in the driver's seat of a black 07 suburban; dro weed smoke was heavy inside. Jim was dressed in all black with a black ski mask on his neck, Plies was playing out the speakers talking about Murkin Season as he waited on Sin to come out the house. Jim's cell rang as Sin was hopping in the truck.

"Yea?" Jim answered his phone

"Yo bra, everybody in position . . . We waiting on ya'll son."

"It's on son." Jim said and hung up.

"That was Springer . . . They all in place." Jim told Sin.

"Let's ride out then sun." Sin said as he sparked a blunt of dro that Jim had in the center console . . .

The ride took about 45 minutes; Jim parked and watched the 3 story house that Hicks lived in. It was Thanksgiving Day and Sin had based his entire plan on detective Hicks being the typical brainwashes piece of shit. He expected his entire family to arrive sometime around 1:00pm to begin the celebrating the theft of a continent. It was a little after 2:00pm and by now they're family should be at the dinner table eating. Sin passed Jim the blunt and put on a pair of black leather gloves before reaching in the back seat to grab one of the two SKS assault rifles, checking the clip he passed it to Jim and grabbed the other one for himself. Jim chirped Shotty to see what was up. Shotty had been staking out Hicks house for hours now. He knew who all was in the house and the layouts of the house.

"Holla at me son." Jim said.

"They all at the dinner table G." Shotty said.

Jim looked at the house that sat a far distance from the street and asked Shotty.

"What direction is that?"

"When you come up to the front, you gotta go to the far left . . . It's a big ass picture window and you'll see them all at the table. We gotta run up fast G." Shotty told Jim.

Sin had heard it all so he knew the plan. Jim and Sin both got out the truck and once Shotty seen them he too hopped out of his rental car and jogged up with a Tec.9 in his hand. As they got closer to the house Jim and Shotty headed towards the big window as Sin went to the front door. Sin stood there adrenaline rushing as he thought of his brother Donta and the pain his mother would feel the rest of her life. Sin took a deep breath then heard machine gun style shots being fired, glass burst and screams of terror erupted. Sin waited till the shots died out before he licked two shots into the door lock, busting it open. Running inside thru the living room and into the dining room Sin seem Hicks wife laid out with multiple gun shots wounds. Hicks two sons were also dead next to their mother, even the family dog was dead. Hicks and his daughter were still alive; he was hovered over her in a protective state.

"What do you want . . . ?" Hicks started to ask as he looked and seen Sin's face answering his own question.

"Get the fuck up." Sin yelled.

Hicks did as he was told just as Jim and Shotty came running through the front door.

"Yo let's go son." Jim said as Hicks daughter yelled out.

"Daddy."

"Come on . . . She coming too." Sin said with his SKS pointed directly at Hicks face. They quickly rushed them outta the house leaving 3 dead bodies for McCoy to find . . .

Two hours later Hicks was tied up to a chair and sprayed with lighter fluid . . . He was barely conscious from the beating he'd been taking and hadn't seen his daughter since they'd been dragged to this abandon building. It was dark, cold and smelled of mildew and Hicks couldn't begin to guess where he was cause the city of Dayton was full of abandon buildings. He started hearing footsteps getting closer and closer then seen Sin approaching with a phone in his hand.

"Whats ya boss number?" Sin asked.

"Where's my little girl?" Hicks yelled.

Sin picked up a bat and smacked Hicks across the knee cap.

"Bitch I'm asking the questions." Sin told Hicks who then yelled out the phone number.

McCoy answered on the second ring and Sin put the phone to Hicks ear.

"Boss." Hicks blurted out but Sin snatched the phone back and heard McCoy saying.

"Hicks where are you . . . My God . . ." Sin cut McCoy off mid sentence though.

"Yo, shut the fuck up and listen . . . We can do this one or two ways. I keep killing your detectives and their families and we keep this war going or you can bring me 5 hundred thousand dollars and 5 kilo's of heroin and clean my name of all the bullshit." Sin said knowing the last request was a far fetch. Sin doubted that he even had a warrant; this war was personal so he knew once he killed McCoy he'd be in the clear. Although he knew they'd be searching for the killer's of the Hicks family high and low. He'd be long gone and their evidence would lead them nowhere.

"Mr. Wallace, listen you've taken things too far. You could get the death penalty for this." McCoy said.

"For what . . . Taking a life. What about how ya'll took my life, I fought to get it back when ya'll tried to bury me with 3 life sentences knowing I wasn't guilty. I beat ya'll legally so ya'll have my brother killed . . . Fuck you and your death penalty. Bitch this is war" Sin spat through the phone.

"Calm down Mr. Wallace. I'm sure we can work something out." McCoy tried to rationalize.

"We don't have shit to work out, do what I ask or your detective and his precious little girl gone die." Sin told McCoy.

"Where the hell am I gonna get a fuckin half a million dollars from? I don't have that kind of money." McCoy told Sin.

Sin placed the phone by Hicks mouth and cracked him across the knee again with the bat causing him to cry out in pain. As Sin pulled the phone back he heard McCoy's plea's.

"Ok, okay . . . Don't kill him . . . Where do we meet?" McCoy asked.

"The old YMCA on route 4 and come by yourself." Sin said and hung up.

Sin had a nice plan that would not only expose these dirty cops but also allow him to get revenge for Donta's death. He also knew that if they got the drop on him he'd be a dead man so he had to be careful . . .

Chapter 21

McCoy was just leaving Hicks house when he'd gotten the call from Sincere Wallace. He was now reasoning with the possibility to try and outsmart Wallace but it was obvious that he wasn't a dummy, he not only had maneuvered through the legal system but he found a way to murder two detective's, one's entire family. He started to realize he had to play Wallace's game, at least long enough to get Hicks and his daughter back safe. Just then he realized his wife and teenage daughter were over his mother-in-laws and panic struck his heart as he quickly called to be sure they were safe. He told his wife to go to a hotel immediately and he'd explain later, then he made a call to detective Flemming.

"Is everything clear at Hicks house?" He asked.

"Yes boss." Flemming replied.

"Ok then . . . I need you to take a ride with me. Meet me at the precinct right now." McCoy said.

"Is everything fine sir?" Flemming asked McCoy knowing it couldn't be after the massacre he just viewed at Hicks house.

"It will be." McCoy said and hung up . . . McCoy decided to take Flemming along to frame him as a dirty cop and then murder Sincere. He'd make it appear that Flemming was stealing from the evidence vault and selling the drugs to Sincere. When he attempted to bust them a shoot occurred and he, Sergeant McCoy would become a hero who brought down this wicked corruption scheme running thru his precinct . . .

McCoy turned the key into the lock of the Evidence and Property Vault; it was after hours and a holiday so the building was almost empty. He went in and began to load up large cubes of money into two duffle bags. Majority of this money and drugs was from raids of drug houses and cases that never went to trial, while other large amounts had been extorted from small and large dealers in the area. McCoy knew he was taking a risk at moving the drugs and money but if the Feds or Internal Affairs ever caught him, he has enough names to give them to receive immunity. After filling two duffle bags and sitting them by the door he called Flemming.

"I'm parking in the garage now sir . . . Do you want me to come up?" Flemming asked after answering the phone.

"Yes, you need to carry these bags." McCoy responded.

When Flemming got to the evidence room McCoy had him grab the two bags to carry to the car and place in the back seat. Flemming had been a part of their crooked cop schemes but never as deep as Hicks, Williams and McCoy so he was curious as to what was going on.

"Boss if you don't mind my asking, what's this all about? I mean does it have anything to do with Hicks?" Flemming asked.

McCoy ignored him as he started the car to leave the precinct. It wasn't until 5 minutes later that McCoy told Flemming all about Sincere Wallace's involvement in the murder of Detective Williams and now Detective Hicks family . . .

* * *

Dru Down watched on top of the roof of a tall building next to the YMCA with Hicks daughter. He had her duct taped up and was waiting on the word from either Sin or Jim. Dru Down watched as a car pulled up and two detective's got out, one opened the back door and pulled out two huge bags. One detective stayed at the car while the other struggled to carry the bags around the building. Dru Down snatched up Hicks daughter and put a .38 Special to her temple.

"Clap." Was all the detective heard. He stopped in his tracks to look around but seen nothing, his next step would be forever be etched in his memory. Dru Down tossed the lifeless girls body over the edge of the roof in the direction of the detective. She burst open like a water balloon as soon as she hit the pavement. McCoy dropped the bags and looked up in fear and disbelief but didn't see anyone, then his phone rang startling him.

"Didn't I tell you to come alone?" The caller who was Sin said.

"Yes, but . . ." McCoy began but was cut off

"Fuck that . . . Go kill your partner or you and Hicks gone die." Sin said and hung up.

McCoy had no win and he knew it but he didn't care, he planned on killing Flemming anyway. McCoy took a deep breath, then left the bags and returned to the car.

"You ok boss?" Flemming asked puffing on a Marlboro cigarette.

McCoy didn't answer; he just drew his 357 Magnum and squeezed 3 shots at his partners head. Pieces of Flemming brain and skull went all over the windshield and without a second thought of what he'd just done McCoy turned to head back around the building. When he made it back around the building, the bags were gone and there laid the lifeless body of Hicks daughter. He looked at this little girl he'd known her whole life and finally realized this war had gone too far. He could see his own daughter's reflection inside this crumpled mess and it began to hurt knowing he'd caused this to happen. As he looked up from his brief trance he seen the long barrel of the SKS assault rifle pointed at him.

"Get the fuck in here." Sin said menacingly.

McCoy cooperated and walked in to the building where a strong stench of lighter fluid burned his nostrils. He felt Sin place the barrel in his back so he knew he had to do something and quick.

"Look... All your money's in the bag... The heroin too." McCoy said as he looked around the room for a possible escape route. Sin didn't speak as he led McCoy further into the building.

"We had a deal." McCoy yelled starting to feel the pressure of the situation. McCoy seen Hicks tied to a chair and barely conscious as he walked into a large room that had a large bathtub in the center of it and 3 other men awaiting him and Sin. McCoy finally knew the deal was null-n-void and him and Hicks were dead men. Sin pulled out a hunting knife and tossed it to Springer and said.

"Kill them both."

McCoy watched in horror as Hicks was stabbed repeatedly in the gut, chest and face. The smell of shit filled the air as Hicks body released his bowels causing McCoy to vomit. Springer started laughing then Sin pushed McCoy towards the tub and told him to,

"Get in and get comfortable bitch."

McCoy looked at the tub and realized it was full of lighter fluid. He was petrified and turned to make a run for the door but was stopped in his tracks when Sin wacked him across the face with his SKS. McCoy had dropped to one knee and as Springer and Jim approached him he was afraid to resist them pulling him to his feet. McCoy continued to plead but it went unanswered and he eventually was laying inside the bathtub. Sin pulled out a book of matches and lit one.

"Please . . . Please . . . Please." McCoy begged but Sin couldn't hear him. All Sin heard was Donta's voice from when they were kid's, how he'd always say he stayed in school cause he didn't wanna die in these streets. Sin's blood was boiling thinking of how his little brother must have been tricked by these pigs before they shot him execution style. Sin had to drop the match cause it had burned down to his finger tips.

"Please . . . What else do you want from me?" McCoy asked Sin but Sin wasn't interested in nothing but his life so he struck another match and dropped it to the ground a few feet ahead of him where it caught fire and lit a trail to the tub setting Detective McCoy ablaze . . .

Chapter 22

I'm Donna Jordan and this is Channel 7 reporting on our top story. I'm on location at the YMCA on route 4 just off of Gettysburg Ave where 3 dead bodies were discovered. Now, the Dayton Police aren't releasing any names but we will tell you that a large amount of money and drugs were found at the scene. We're told this appears to have been a drug deal gone awfully wrong and also appears connected to the horrendous massacre of the family of a detective Dewayne Hicks earlier today . . .

Sin clicked off the t.v and thought of how it was gonna be around here while they attempted to untangle this mess. Sin had cleaned up the scene then left $100,000 and 1 kilo of heroin busted open around the doorway to where Hicks and McCoy were dead at. The other 4 kilo's and $400,000 had went to Jim, Springer, Shotty and Dru Down to be divided up.

"Daddy hurry up." Infinity said running into the front room. Sin grabbed his daughter's suitcase and said.

"Why are you ready?"

"Yes daddy come on." Infinity said.

"Come on princess." Sin said motioning to his daughter.

"How long you gonna be gone with my baby?" Kia asked standing in the doorway.

"I'ma keep her till she ready to come back . . . At least till school start back right baby." Sin told Kia and then his daughter.

"Aight ma we out . . . You know I'm laying low so I'll let you know where we at once we get settled in." Sin told Kia as him and his daughter headed out the door . . .

* * *

Sin ended up in Atlanta where he brought his own condo and had his son and daughter's come stay with him every summer. He kept up with the investigation via the internet and after a whole year it was still a mystery as to who had committed the "Thanksgiving Massacre's" as they had been daubed by the media. Sin had no police looking for him and no petty street wars to watch out for cause he was no longer hustling illegally. With over $500,000 stashed Sin focused heavy on his music, he had lived what all rappers were rapping about, so why not tell his story. It was 100% authentic and his skills on the mic painted the picture of his life. Sin had a drive beyond any of his competition; his little brother was living thru him so he went extra hard. It didn't take long for Sin to get a deal worth 7 figures and put out mix tape after mix tape full of heat to build his buzz. While others didn't live it, they witnessed it from their windows, wrote it in their note pads and created their lives; Sin had not only lived it but mastered it. And now you couldn't mention his city unless you mentioned his name . . .

Sincere Wallace was Street Royalty all throughout the 937 . . . .

Street Royalty 937
Part 2: Seven Takes Over

PREFACE

Like every other hood ni$$a, money and a way out was Seven's motivation. To live like the dope boys on his block, to rock shines like them, to fuck bad bitches like them, drive the fliest whips and count rubber band bank rolls like them. But unlike most, after seeing all the streets had to offer and how they'd taken his mother outta his life he repelled to some parts of the street life. It was in his blood line to master the pistol play and hustle but he was wise beyond his years due to the time he'd spent up under Sincere who was running the streets when Seven was a kid...That alone had attracted the attention of two of the biggest dope boys in the city and gave him the chance to get down with them at a young age. Soon signals would get crossed with their out of town connect and Shorty found himself in a position of power. One trip and he was now running the city. But with more money, comes larceny from people you've never even met. After two of the biggest coke+heroin connects take a fall could Seven handle the pressure of the target being on his back or would he fold to the older hustler's who had no problem robbing+murdering in order to get his spot. Who can you trust when it becomes known that your holding millions in your stash. Seven would soon find out the hard way and the consequences that came with being Street Royalty in the 937...

Chapter 1

Gunshots rang out somewhere close to Seven's house but it wasn't shit unusual about that. It was actually common on his block. This Desoto Bass Projects but better known as "The Bass" and it still held its reputation as one of the rawest blocks throughout Dayton, Ohio. Seven was up late like always on a school night watching the cartoon network. Old episodes of Scooby Doo were on and he was laughing while he watched and ate a bowl of Fruity Pebbles cereal when his mom came into the room.

"Seven, don't forget to take out the trash before you got to bed." Seven's mom Cat said.

"Aight mom," he answered back still focused on the t.v screen. Ten minutes later Seven was unlocking the back door with the trash in hand. It took his eye's a second or two to adjust to the darkness outside but once he did he stood there stuck. Laying at the bottom of the back steps was a dead body. A young ni$$a around 18 or 19 years old had gotten half his face blown off. Seven dropped the trash where he stood and managed to take his eyes off the body and went back into the house. His heart raced with fear and his mind was confused on whether to run tell his mom or not. He was only 8 years old but had already heard of ni$$az getting shot up just had never seen the aftermath of it. Calming down Seven found himself a little curious so he stared out the door window at the dead body with crazy thoughts running through his head about why it had happened. Leaving the trash by the door Seven headed to his room still playing back scenario's in his head until he fell asleep. A short time later he was awaken by the loud sirens and paramedic radios. Police were going door to door lookin for answers but talking to the police was a death sentence in his hood. Everyone knew the codes of the hood and if the police stayed at one door longer than necessary, then somebody would be to see about them. It was funny like that in the hood and the city's police knew it, so after only an hour of investigating this murder they left with no leads, no cooperation, and not one suspect. Although the truth was all over the hood in a matter of days, even Seven knew the ni$$a had got his head popped off over $700 he owed, the police would never be able to prove it...

It had been 12 years since Seven had seen his first dead body and he'd been immune ever since. Living in "The Bass" was rough for Seven growing up but when he was 11 years old his moms had started fucking with this fly ass ni$$a name Sin and shit started to change. Money started to flow in and they moved out the projects and to the Upper View section of Dayton but Seven never really seen his moms anymore and although he loved Sin's style and he looked up to him, he started to resent his moms and the shit she was into. Seven knew his mom was a stripper and that she'd set up ni$$a's who was getting money for Sin to rob them. At 12 years old Seven would always try to mimick Sin's style, his lingo, and his mom hated that, so Seven hit the streets hard to avoid seeing his mom on a regular basis. Sin would always pick Seven up whenever he was in town checking his trap houses. They'd ride around for hours and Sin would always test Seven on things he's taught him on prior occasions. Seven learned a lot of knowledge about life in general from Sin. He would tell Seven that once you learned about who you were, everything else would come easily especially the streets. Seven soaked up Sin's wise words for a year straight before Sin had caught three life sentences and disappeared. Seven had written Sin a few times but he knew Sin was busy fighting his appeal. By the time Sin won his appeal and hit the streets again, Seven was doing a juvenile bid in Mawame, Ohio so they missed each other. Seven heard Sin had the city on smash when he came home, but a lot had jumped off causing him to leave Ohio before Seven was released on his 18th birthday...

Chapter 2

I be thuggin and it ain't no secret...Some old B.G Cash Money shit banged low in Seven's Q45 Infinity as he sparked up a blunt of Kush on his way to meet his old heads name Demon and Steph at the carwash on Gettysburg. Demon and Steph had been handling bricks in Springfield since the late 80's before Seven was born. They'd both did a 10 year bid at separate times and since their releases had been hustling in Dayton. Although they had 20 years on Seven they still had mad love for him and his hustle, plus he looked just like a young Sincere who they used to fuck with before doing their time. They'd always fuck with Seven and say he was Sin's son. Seven didn't mind cause he had mad love for Sin but he ain't think Sin was his father his mom even told him he wasn't Sin's son.

Seven was still reppin the most feared hood in the city, Desoto Bass, which was known for bodying outsiders and outta towner's. His hood was after straight blood money and was infamous for it in the streets. Demon and Steph still never thought twice about embracing Seven and his connection to his hood, they'd been in the streets long enough to know who's who and what's what. Seven had a mean hustle hand and whenever he put in work in the streets he wasn't your average young reckless little ni$$az who been out here years before him. Seven had polish so it was only natural that he is touching some paper but the paper ain't change him. The bottles he popped in the club every weekend, the studs in his ear worth 5 stacks, the chain and watch with at least 37 karat's in clear diamonds, none of the could change Seven. Regardless of the work he had or money he counted, Seven was still Seven, 5ft 6 inches, 160ibs, and stocky, brown skin, with wavy hair. A pretty boy type ni$$a at first glance but wasn't shit pretty for real, he had the persona of a boss but the heart of a goon...

As Seven turned into the carwash he seen Demon's Cranberry 87 Deuce and a Quarter. Everything Demon touched from bitches to whips and jewelry to the clothes he rocked was always exclusive. Today he had on all-white Prada linen fit with some off white Suede Prada dress shoes. Steph was the total opposite, he kept some crisp braids and a fresh pair of kicks but every T-shirt, which was the only thing he wore, kept some type of stain on them. Whenever people heard about Steph they expected to meet a flashy ni$$a cause everyone knew he was caked up but that wasn't his style and Seven kinda liked that about his old head. Seven hopped out his whip dressed in some smoked grey sweats, white and grey Educated Thug Wear T-shirt, grey fitted cap, and some gray and white retro Jordan's.

"What's poppin?" Seven said to the two as he gave them both dapps and hugs.

"Shit, what it do young'n?" Steph said to Seven.

"What it look like over there?" Demon asked speaking on the weed spot on Brooklyn Ave they'd just opened up a few weeks ago. They'd planned a 30 day run before they were gonna close shop, it had been jumpin already and clientele and to much more traffic would have the spot hot. That's how they moved, so by the time the police got wind of the spot the money would be made and ni$$az was M.I.A with it.

"Shit, I got bout 3lbs Kush and 4lbs of purple left. I ain't got no dro or no reg." Seven said as he took a long drag on the Kush he was smoking.

"Damn you ran through that shit!" Steph said as Demon asked.

"It was 10lbs of everything right?"

"Yea." Seven said passin the weed to Steph. Demon quickly did the math.

"What's that bout $200...a little over $200,000?" Demon asked.

"$220,400 in 3 weeks, what you know about that." Seven said. I'm off'n that Kush $10,400 a pound, that purp went for $9,600 and I kept that dro and reg the same ticket as always." Seven told them.

"That's what's up, you keep $100,000 and I'll pick up the rest later. Johnny got the house on Clark St ready, he's a week early but I told him I'd call him back." Steph told Seven.

Johnny was a realtor who had a heroin addiction, him and his family owned property on both the east and west side of Dayton. Johnny would set up spots for Demon and Steph in exchange for heroin or powder, money was often exchanged but rarely. Johnny mostly preferred product and he was also their direct link to a lot of the upscale clientele on the east side of town where the white people stayed. The average lawyer, public defender, doctor and the nurse all lived out there and most had some type of addiction. One time while out east meeting a young white bitch at the Golden Corral, Seven recognized a judge he'd went in front of on driving under a suspension charge. Turns out the judge liked to snort coke with young hoes and now that Seven had him on his clientele he intended to put him to use in the future. If he ever got caught up in some shit out that way one call to him could make it disappear.

"The house on Clark St is just where we're stashin work and postin up, we gone grind out of White Pine Apartments. We gotta get off 2 bricks of heroin and 3 bricks of coke, that's too much for the new homes." Steph was saying.

"Them apartments in White Pine, they Johnny's?" Demon asked.

"Nah they official though. I'm trying to make $500,000 off this move. I got some white boys out there and a few white hoes so I'll slide out there today and make sure shit still official." Steph said.

"That all sound good but what's poppin in the hoods lately? Shorty asked Steph.

"Same ole shit young'n its murkin season." Steph replied.

Ever since they'd open the spot on Brooklyn Ave Seven hadn't made any rounds thru the hoods in the city. He'd been posted try'n to move all 50 pounds Demon and Steph had dumped on him.

"What you talkin bout?" Seven asked.

"Some clowns ni$$a done opened a weed spot on Alpena." Demon said.

"Oh yea, who is he?" Seven asked.

"What difference do that make, he ain't from the hood." Demon said matter factly.

Just then Seven's phone rang so he took a few steps away to answer it while Demon and Steph continued talking.

"What's good ma." Seven answered

"You...what's jumpin daddy." Dallas said in a sexy voice.

"I'm just out and about how you been ma." Seven asked.

"Well if you out and about you can come see me!" Dallas said.

"Why what you on ma?" Seven said with a light laugh cause he knew what Dallas was up too. She was just a fuck thing and every time she called that's what she wanted.

"I want to taste you daddy." Dallas said as sexy as she could.

"Oh yea...It's on then ma just give me a minute and I'll call you back." Seven told Dallas, then hung up and returned his attention to Demon and Steph,

"On Alpena huh" Seven said looking at Demon and Steph." I'ma look into that." Seven said as he gave both his ni$$az dap.

"You gone young'n?" Steph asked.

"Yea, I'ma holla back later." Seven said as he jumped in his whip.

As Seven drove to Dallas house he thought about the last time he fucked with her. It was about 3 weeks ago a day or two before he opened up on Brooklyn Ave. She had come through on Sweetest Day and took Seven to the Marriot. She had the room set up with rose pedals sprinkled all around the floor and bed that was surrounded by scented candles. She even had a few bottles of Rose Moet and a sack of dro weed for Seven to relax with. Seven actually dug this little bitch, she was about 5ft 7 inch tall and 160 pounds with caramel complexion that matched her eye color. She had small titties with a phat phat ass that was super soft every time Seven squeezed it. She'd finished college last year and now worked at a bank downtown in the Mulligan Building. Seven never fucked with her heavy or wifed her cause he knew as long as he was in the streets getting money and staying on his shit bitches would always be at him. Some of the baddest hoes in the oddest places would go out of their way to talk to Seven or try to slide him a number or address without even knowing who he was, just cause he looked like money. Seven knew how scandalous these hoes could be, he'd seen it first hand in his own mother's actions. Therefore Seven trusted none of these bitches that try'd to holla at him. Dallas was no different in his eyes out of the many times he'd fucked he never once initiated sex so she was another dope boys dick friend in his eyes. Seven's train of thought was broke as he turned on Dallas street and flew past her house. He had no intentions on calling her back earlier he preferred to just show up on his own time so it'll be harder for him to set up to be robbed. After circling the block Seven pulled into Dallas driveway and hit his horn twice. Dallas opened the door in a silk robe and said

"What's up daddy." as Shorty got out his whip.

"Ain't nothing ma coming to see if I can get you wet?" Seven said as he stepped in the house closing the door behind him.

They kissed for a minute before Dallas dropped her robe to the floor, then pulled off Seven's hat and T-shirt. Dallas pushed Seven down on the couch, then kneeled down in front of him on her knees. She began to pull his sweat pants from under him as she looked directly at him and licked her lips seductively. Seven was semi hard but as she grabbed his dick with both hands it grew before her eyes making her want to suck him even more. She put her mouth around his dick head and teased him a little before bobbing down on as much of his dick as she could handle. After 5 minutes she could tell he was about to cum cause he began to tense up and lift his hips to meet her mouth. Dallas started to suck with more aggression causing Seven to explode in her mouth but like a pro she kept sucking and swallowing all at once leaving no trace of cum when she was done.

Standing up Dallas took Seven's hand and let him upstairs to the bedroom. Seven had kicked off his sweats on the way after he grabbed a condom out of his pocket. In the room Seven told Dallas to lay down while he strapped up, then grabbed her ankles and pushed them back to her head before entering her. She let out a loud moan as Seven slid deeper and deeper into her pussy..."Ahh...Oh shit" She screamed as he started to thrust harder. Seven beat her pussy up for 10 minutes before he told her to turn around so he could hit her from the back. Dallas flipped over and put her phat ass in the air and placed her face in the pillow. Seven slid inside her from the back held her waist and started to bang into her pussy real hard and fast. She tried to bite into the pillow to muffle her screams but it didn't help, tears started to run down her face as she yelled out in ecstasy. "Fuck me...fuck me...oh shit ooh ssshittt...I'm cuming....Oh daddy slow down...oh shit." Dallas yelled as Seven held her hips and fucked her with reckless abandon. Dallas knees finally buckled and she fell flat in her stomach as Seven remained inside her he began to grind slow and kiss and suck on her neck and shoulder. Seven felt his nut cumming so he grabbed her shoulders and dug deep as he busted and filled up the condom. Dallas moaned in pleasure as Seven slowed his strokes to a stop and went limp inside of her.

A half hour of pillow talk and half a blunt later Seven got up to go wash up and get dressed.

"Damn I see somebody in a rush." Dallas said irritatedly.

"Nah ma get dressed and spin the block with me." Seven said putting on his hat.

They drove around the city for an hour or so talkin about a little bit of everything, stopping in different hoods and fucking with a few ni$$az before Seven pulled onto Alpena St. He pulled out a $50 bill and said, "Go in there and get some weed."

"How much?" She asked

"Spend all of it ma." Seven told her as she got out the car.

Seven watched as Dallas knocked on the door and Seven watched as Dallas knocked on the door and a skinny brown skinned ni$$a opened it with a smile on his face. She was only inside about 2 or 3 minutes before she emerged and walked to the car. As she got back in Seven asked

"How many ni$$az was in there?"

"Just the one I think why is there something wrong?" Dallas said curious.

"Nah ma shit is all good." Seven said as he pulled off never making eye contact.

That was all he needed to know cause he was planning on some in and out shit. He dropped Dallas off and headed back to Alpena Ave within 10 minutes hoping nobody else had came through since he'd left cause they'd get it too. Seven pulled up to the house and it appeared that nobody else had came by so he headed to the door and knocked. The same skinny brown skinned ni$$a answered.

"What's good fam?" He asked as he let Seven in like any other customer.

It's over for this stupid ass ni$$a Seven though to his self.

"Let me get a $20 bag." Seven said.

"It's on fam." He answered as he went behind a desk and opened a side drawer to pull out the $20. "Here you go fam" he said.

"Do you got dro, that's all I smoke for real. I got $50 for some dro." Seven said. The ni$$a got geeked up and took his eyes off Shorty just long enough for Seven to go for his .38 special revolver or what homeboy thought was his money. "Boom Boom" Seven shot him twice in the side of his head causing brain fragments to smack the wall before his body hit the floor. On instinct Seven walked around the desk where he seen a blue duffel, which he used to dump all the contents of each drawer into. Making his way to his whip he sped off towards one of his 3 storage units after being sure he wasn't followed he pulled into the unit where he counted the money and pounds of weed. As Seven changed whips he laughed to his self at how this dumb ass ni$$a had got his self killed over 11 pounds and 16 stacks. Even though money or robbery wasn't the reason Seven had killed him it was still funny. He was in another ni$$az hood try'n to get it like he was official out here. Half the ni$$az out here had to shoot something early and often to keep their positions solidified so how was this nothing ass ni$$a expecting to survive.

Seven stopped by his aunt's house to change clothes real quick before he went back to the hood. He pulled up in front of Gebharts Corner Store where Demon and Steph sat in Demon's whip. Seven hopped out and walked into the store to get some blunt wraps and an Ever Fresh orange juice. When he came out a few minutes later he hopped in Demon's back seat and said "What's good?"

"Ain't shit its hot ass fuck out here young'n." Steph said.

"Yea I seen a few unmarked cars lunkin around." Seven said looking out the window.

"They found that fuck ni$$a leanin with 4 or 5 to the head." Demon said as he turned to look at Seven's expression.

Seven looked at Steph and he could tell that they both had it on they minds.

"Nah...The bitch ass ni$$a only got hit twice." Seven said as he leaned back knowing he'd took it off his old heads mind and they'd never talk about that again.

CPSIA information can be obtained at www.ICGtesting.com
Printed in the USA
BVOW021244240712

296066BV00003B/23/P